The Ageless of Aquarius

{Being the Second Tale in
A Measure of Poe & Three Quarters}

Steven Mooney

Steven Mooney Books
Olympia, Washington

ISBN: 978-1-7345356-7-9
Library of Congress Control Number: 2020905126
Cover Art & Design by Jessica Bell Design
Published by Steven Mooney Books

For Dina

I removed all resistance until I floated in my own invention.
– Thomas McGuane

No one interested in how newspaper reporters find their stories should imagine that the compass needle is reset each time out. What they find attractive doesn't change, only where they find it.
– Pete Dexter

Book One

The Mystic Knights of Moonstone Light

Can a mountain sing? Sightless, she scrambled on hands and knees as the chanting grew from faint hint to rhythmic signal and she pawed toward a Gregorian echo that pierced the core of Mt. Gertrude. Led onward by sound alone she bumped stone and then became frantic, unable to find egress in the Cimmerian cavern, but calmed herself with yogic breath, so that after crawling about and bumping a few more walls she found the twigs she had dropped to mark her way and at last saw the oriel of light and shoveled herself out of the mouth, to sit beside the cave in dappled sunlight where more familiar voices caught her attention, wind and birds, but she knew she'd be back, even if she got lost in there, she'd be back as soon as she could and she vowed to do so as she rode her bike down the trail toward Rainbow Run. In the loft she lay on her futon under dust motes dancing in prisms louvered in layers of stained-glass sunlight from an oriel they called the mandala, and she extemporized what she'd heard from the cave in a poetic sketch and got back into Pearl, her current spiritual advisor. An hour later with the vibe from the cave merely a footnote, she opened the shop and put her bike behind the counter of the communal store where her family sold second-hand clothes, candles, bead ware, organic snacks, crystals, and gemstones too. An ordinary Saturday would find her here at Blue Jay Way until sundown, but today was gonna be different, and after she hung the flag stop banner, she perched on a stool behind the counter, too excited about the bus and the impending event to read the book of poems in her bag.

~ ~ ~

Sprawled on the car, Jam resembled a cartoon bug in his stained mechanic's jumpsuit, one leg across a quarter-panel and the other skewed over the radiator. Double-jointed in the hips, he could lay atop an engine compartment like a boomerang. That day he worked on the relic Rambler station wagon, an appropriately named car for over the years they had rambled together, his mobile workshop, as he'd operated on every piece of equipment they owned and some they didn't, like his stint at one of the garages in town just to have fun tinkering.

He'd come south with Cody and the bunch back in, what was it 66, 67 when everybody said they were crazy: the south was just an endless swamp of racists and rednecks. Well, sure there were hassles in the early years, a couple of raids by the sheriff, and townies treating them badly, but eventually, and it didn't take too long, and who really counted or cared, these hippies were community. Mountain-folk often perceive themselves as outcasts, and as the hamlet of Round Wilson had grown into a bona fide Appalachian crossroads, the commune sod busters blended with the other farmers down in the valley, and folks became folks.

These days many a farmer could thank the commune hippies for the free help they'd offered, yes, free, in clearing fields, cutting and hauling wood, bringing in the harvest, herding wayward cattle, as well as barn loads of advice on ahead-of-its-time organic farming. Jam's finest hour was when he had overhauled the town's fleet of two school buses in exchange for a wagonload of dung. Ah, but that manure grew the greatest gold he'd ever rolled!

Swiveling off the Rambler, he fired up the engine and squatted on his heels to listen. He could sit this way for hours, as natural to him as the earth on which he did most of his work. Other mechanics needed tables and benches, but Jam would lay out a square of waxed cardboard, sit on his heels, and go to work, as often beside his rolling garage, the Rambler wagon whose engine purred like it had the day it rolled off a Detroit assembly line, and now this strange looking hunk of steel and chrome was once again ready to open a window on style, as well as get him over the mountain. He parked the car and went to wash up, hedging other jobs on the wait-list, but what was a wait-list for? He examined his beard, where recently he'd found two ladybugs in the red and the gray mesh. While he thought it was cool that they would hang out there, man, a free ride, you gotta dig that action, he was concerned about ticks. So, here's this old face, aging sure is weird; look the same; narrow mug, hawk nose, but this gray is wild; it's haiku in action, man and his thoughts turned to Button, her coal black hair everywhere, her brilliance, and of his oldest friends, her parents, who at that moment were sitting down to lunch.

~ ~ ~

Cody brought the bowl of mashed potatoes and dill weed to the table where his partner of thirty years and common law wife was already digging in.

"Hey, sorry I ragged you about going with her, I think she needs her space, you know?"

Cody loaded his plate before replying. "Well, like she said, let her do her own thing, if she wanted us tagging along, she'd have asked. She's old enough to handle herself. Hell, wiser than either of us at her age. Besides, she needs an adventure." He squeezed lemon juice onto his salad greens. Amanda was already loading up seconds and it reminded him of how she'd really gained weight the last several years; given their lifestyle it didn't seem to make sense.

"Jam was truly sorry he couldn't drive her down. He really wanted to see her get glorified," said Cody, mopping up bean sauce with a nugget of bread.

"I hate buses like those. I'd settle for Jam any day," said Amanda, forking another veggie burger off the tray.

"Well, he had some important business up toward Johnson City."

"Some kind of bubble, what's that about?"

"It's not a bubble, baby, it's a nosecone from some bomber."

"A bomber? An airplane?"

"Well, it ain't the one *we* know, speaking of which, I haven't had time to burn one all day. He left the table and returned with an apple, lifted the stem and pulled out cigarette papers and began to roll a smoke. "Or those other bombs?" she said, recalling her Psych pal Claire whispering 'he's in the SDS.' Cody looked her dead in the eye.

"We agreed way back we'd never mention that, never so much as even a breath about it. We've got it too good here, babe." Their eyes held.

"Sorry, hon, it's just the topic; I don't want Jam bringing death onto this farm."

"I don't think there's symbolism enough there to warrant concern, it's just a piece of glass," said Cody, lighting his cigarette. "Besides, that stupid war ranged a lot of people."

"You gonna have any carrot cake?" she asked as he handed her the joint.

"In about an hour I'll eat the whole thing," and they shared a good laugh.

2

As the bus coughed and hacked to crawl around a switchback, Button peered over the edge, over the broccoli-tops to where the horizon sat in azure fog. Where the Blue Ridge got its name, she said aloud. She'd been down this road only once before when she'd gone with Cody and Jam and Amanda to Winston-Salem and spent the day on the cracked mud of junkyards. Later she had written a short story about that experience (her father had an eye for salvage that rivaled none). In her story, "Wipe-out Paradise," a pack of unionized junkyard dogs were having a labor dispute with a high-tech management team that wanted to turn the salvage yard into an automotive Memory Lane and drive-in theatre where they'd show all the great car-chase movies. Her family, by which she meant everyone in the commune, had praised her story, except Jam, who cautioned her that in these parts the term *union* was received about as kindly as *devil*, and advised that she send her story up north. *Jam.* She'd known him all of her life and next to Cody he was better than uncle, a second dad.

The bus descended the foothills and passed through small towns built like strip malls alongside the road. Button thought the houses looked tawdry and imagined the people inside them were either haunted in loneliness or argued about vacuum cleaners. Too bad Jam had to go to Tennessee this weekend or he would have given me a ride, she lamented, before digging her latest Toni Morrison out of her bag and stretching across the empty seat. Soon she saw the folly in trying to concentrate: tonight's gonna be a kick, and she wondered where that junkyard was in proximity to her present destination in Cig City.

~ ~ ~

From the speech to applause to reading to award and more reading, Button couldn't keep her mind on the proceedings of the Regional Writing Awards. She came in and out of the ceremony, listening rapt to one reader and then sliding off somewhere and she knew she had a wombat but couldn't stop it any more than she could swim in the carpet. She'd picked up the expression at home and regardless of what it meant used it like a sort of mantra. One spring day as she rode her pony beneath a patchwork quilt of lumpy clouds, she chanced to hear Jam exclaim: "No wonder I couldn't set her in there, I had me a wombat." She adopted this bit of mysticism the way only a child can, inventing talisman and tuning in the chakras of the soul.

Thus, when she heard her name she drifted down from her balloon ride and further down the aisle to the stage and got into her reading, and when asked by a judge to read another poem, she really dug the attention, a lake of heads rapt on every word and phrase, yet she sensed that the enormity of the room rendered the poem insignificant within the strength it needed to command a measure of space.

The space for the reception was less commanding, as long tables strung with bunting sectioned Beverage from Hors d'oeuvre. Unaccustomed to crowds and a bit freaked by the swarming lobby and the penumbra of combatant perfumery, she strove to evade but alas, was buttonholed between the steam tables and the finger food. She gave in, but took in as payment goofy sidelong leers at her bulbous reflection in the burnished sheen of coffee urns. Moving on amid the swirl of writers and media, she found herself holding a saucer of tea sandwiches, and when she peeled back a wedge of sourdough to see what lay beneath, she lost her cool. "Oh Gross," she was heard to remark as she shoved the dish into the hands of a man, and tried to flee, but the recipient, proffering the snack before him like a waiter, cornered her by a Fichus tree that cast its faux shade beneath the fluorescent sky.

"Excuse me, miss, but I wanted to speak with you."

"You shouldn't eat that; you are what you eat is the first rule of life," she declared.

"Miss Springfield, I'm—"

"Your wig is slipping, and you get that *death* out of here." As he emptied the plate into the planter his hairpiece went with it. He restored it and furtively glanced about as Button sought to determine the higher level of absurdity: diced dead pig on a platter or a man with two heads of hair.

"Miss Springfield, I hope you'll excuse me. My name is Del Mabler. I thought your poems were beautiful, and so did my boy who," and he craned his neck, "is here somewhere."

Something about his broad nose and puffy lips made him seem oddly familiar to her. "Wasn't there a Ray Mabler tonight?"

"That's my son. He won third place in Sci-fi. We're very proud of him."

At that moment they were joined by the journalist Tarleton Ramseur and a young man who filled the remaining space in that corner. Ramseur introduced himself and then his protégé, and she smiled at Randal Poe.

"*The Mountain News*, yeah I've seen that around," said Button.

"We're up that way too, Nettles, about ten miles from Ms. Springfield's Round Wilson," said Mabler who, caught by Ramseur's glare, tried to back away.

"I know it," said Button but offered nothing more as she flashed her last visit with her mom. It had been raining ice and the doctor's office smelled like a hog farm.

"Ms. Springfield," said Mabler, "your folks are here too?"

"I came on the bus."

"Well, we'd be happy to offer you a ride, if you like," he said, and excused himself to go search for his son, trailed by Ramseur, while the young journalist chatted with Button.

"Excuse me sir, may I have a word with you? You may not recall it, but we have met before." Mabler waited, fidgeting, eyeing Ramseur.

"Six years ago, if I'm not mistaken, you reneged on an interview, but I caught you sneaking out of that hotel kitchen."

Mabler knew he was cornered. There had been times when he could wiggle and he'd become proficient at it, never more than a tablecloth away from invisible, but not this time, not with family in tow.

"Well, uh, yes, uh, what is it you want?"

"You've quite disappeared have you not? Vanished off the face of the earth, it'd be fair to say. Ordinarily, when a star of your magnitude falls, it leaves a trace which, if nothing else, grants the multitudes a chance to say, *farewell*."

"Look Mr. Ramseur, I'm sorry about that incident in Memphis, but I had to get out fast."

"A liaison gone awry?"

"Something similar but, it's like this: I have retired."

"Why the disappearing act, then. What was the point of such histrionics?" said Ramseur, as he eyed a plate of barbeque go by. He'd grazed from the tables but only enough to strike up the band of his appetite, and such a warm up was usually the prelude to a concert.

"I think I've said enough." Mabler moved, but a step by Ramseur blocked him with bulk.

"What you fail to realize is that you left everyone hanging, sir, in the lurch. In short, you hurt the people who deserved it the least." Mabler dropped his head and a sigh escaped him like a leaking tire.

"What do you want me to do, then?"

"Tell your story, sir, come out of the dark."

"You don't understand what's at stake."

"Besides, you're a newspaperman, you'll end up spilling the beans and I'll be ruined, again!" Tarleton patted his shoulder, touched by visible despair, and offered conciliation.

"Tell you what, you give me the lowdown and if I print it, and I say *if*, I'll omit your whereabouts and other vital details. The public, especially your public, has a right to know. They don't, however, need to know your phone number," assured Ramseur.

"I'll trust you Ramseur, but not because I think it's a wise idea. You come and see me next weekend," and arrangements were drawn up. Mabler then faded into the crowd to collect his family and return to his mountain home.

During the drive, Ray and Button talked about writing and the forthcoming publication of their work, but the boy was awkward and uncomfortable with criticism, compounded for Button in the company of his parents, but then she was just plain uncomfortable with science fiction. Cody's dog- eared copy of *The Illustrated Man* had left her feeling that all other plots could only be pie pan flying saucers. She wouldn't deny that the genre marched to a different drummer, but it was her conviction that the drummer was a geek, and she pined for an opportunity to ask Mabler about the wig and also why he wore a fake mustache. It was even weirder that his family didn't say something. OK, dad, you can remove the costume now. But then, families did read from the same script, but Cody and Samantha had raised her in a frank and open environment that engendered a spirit uninhibited by many a social constraint. It was marveled by her parents through the years that they had successfully passed on the major elements of their iconoclastic lifestyle. Button was relieved when they rolled into a Texaco and she'd be freed from the restraints of the car. She seized the moment when the mom and son went inside and Mabler was alone, pumping gas. Just wondering, she said, really aching to know. When he didn't respond she guessed, incorrectly, that he hadn't heard amid the din of traffic. She repeated her question. He glared at her for a highway minute.

"Well, I must be losing my touch. Twice in one day. I'll tell you only this much: Federal Witness Protection Program. My family's sworn to secrecy, and so must you be."

"That's like where you're . . . Wow! Well, you have my word, Mr. Mabler. I won't tell a soul, but you listen up, too! F'you ever need any help at all, come over to Rainbow Run, here's the store too," and she handed him the business card for Blue Jay Way. "We have a whole lot of land up there; and you could be a modernized Rip Van Winkle." They shook on it. It seemed the father was far more interesting than the son, especially once he clambered into the back seat with a packet of beef jerky. Fortunately for the sake of demeanor, he didn't offer her any. Oh wow, wait 'til Amanda hears about this, thought Button, a dried-cowhide-licking science-fiction boy. But the other boy she'd met that evening, the journalist, had had an altogether different effect on her.

3

Tarleton Ramseur contemplated historic place names as he drove through the western counties that had initially refused to secede along with the rest of the state as the drums of civil war rumbled like thunder over the peaks and valleys of the old north state. Drumming his fingers on the steering wheel in the parking lot of a fast-food joint he glanced again at the map that showed Nettles and Round Wilson about a thumb-width from Sparta on a looping secondary road near the Tennessee line. Randal returned to the car and handed him a bag: the aroma of hot bacon shuttled Tarleton back to his paper's coverage of the ravages of Hurricane Floyd on Coastal Plain hog farms and the awful mess that was: thousands of drowned pigs in a flood of Biblical proportions flushing sewage polluted floodwater into the estuaries of the Albemarle and Pamlico sounds like the plumes of a gargantuan grunt. He came to in time to exit the interstate and head up a winding two-lane and after an hour he slowed to a speed trap crawl to take in Round Wilson at a glance: the town was three blocks long by two wide and stretched along a ridge and in a moment, they were ascending onward to Nettles where he failed to spot the road Mabler had given him, but then at the top of a rise was a store. Varnish, tobacco, and vegetable aromas assaulted him as he opened the door.

"Sorry, phone's out," offered the clerk.

"Local, maybes I know 'em."

"Nope, long distance, Hong Kong I'm afraid," replied Tarleton, grinning.

"Hong Kong?"

"Business you know. Sampan awnings are up one and a quarter." He found Randal sprawled in the bed of the pickup tilting an outsized box of Cracker Jack.

"Tell me, what do you get for a prize in a box that big?" asked Tarleton.

"This one I get a Sampan awning. You deceived that man."

"Well, heh, sometimes I just fall into these roles. I don't rehearse them. But you have a point; I should be both forthright and sincere." He nodded at the boy. "Nonetheless, I have trouble taking anyone seriously that holds a pound of tobacco in his mouth when he speaks.

Did you note that rivulet? It was like the trailing edge of a squeegee."

After locating the gravel road and running its switchbacks, they arrived at a mud-brown double-wide on a bare lot. The trailer and the ground it sat on were so color coordinated that the curtained windows were the only feature that distinguished one from the other. The door opened on a chain and an eye appeared in the crack.

"Who's he?"

"And good morning to you, sir," replied Tarleton. "I'd like to introduce you to my assistant, Mr. Poe.

"This isn't what we agreed on. I won't be tricked," said Mabler, closing the door, only to find a ballpoint pen in the way. He opened it again to the eye revealing inch.

"If I remember correctly, there was a certain gentleman who gave you a helping hand when you were just starting out. My assistant was pulled from death's door a few years back and I've put him under my wing."

Mabler seated them in the living room, excused himself, and returned a moment later brandishing a tape recorder: "For my protection."

"A little light would help," said Tarleton as Randal thought: fire sale furniture.

"First off, let me tell this: now Elvis was a southerner, like me. I don't think on him as a saint, mind you, but just the finest example of a homeboy you're ever going to get. But you see, all the fan worship drove us both to cover. Another thing, it wasn't southerners who turned Elvis into a god, no sir. We got better sense. It was Yankees that made him into some kind of idol. That ought to tell you why I'm holed up incognito."

Tarleton recalled the headlines he'd written: *Leading Elvis Impersonator Vanishes.* That scoop had boosted that reporter right along, and if Randal played his cards right, this could be his ticket.

"I guess you must be resentful then, driven out of your livelihood and forced into retirement," stated Tarleton.

"On a bad day I'd say that's true. But with time I find that the romantic aspects are becoming prominent in recollection, and the truly bad parts are diminishing."

"What sort of bad parts, sir?"

"The beat-all worst was all them peanut butter and banana sandwiches."

"I thought that—"

"I got so sick of 'em I had to get therapy," said Mabler.

"Well, binge eaters have been known to seek counseling," encouraged the veteran reporter.

"This was different. First, I tried hypnosis. It didn't help. The medium claimed she heard a heavenly choir singing to her from Heartbreak Hotel. Next, I tried a shrink, but that jackass reached so deep into Freud he rang his bellybutton from inside."

"Can you elaborate on that, please?"

"He wanted me to grasp peanut butter and banana as manifestations of repressed sexuality; he was a sick man."

"It sounds as though counseling wasn't doing you much good."

"Well, that was the point where I realized my approach was all wrong. Listen, you guys want some coffee or something?"

When he was out of the room, Tarleton offered Randal quick pointers on interview technique and some background on their host's flight from the limelight. Mabler returned with coffee cups and packets of Instant.

"It wasn't all fans, though. The biggest pests were other impersonators, up and coming, you know? They all wanted tips and guidance because they knew I'd gotten mine directly from The King." For Randal's benefit he explained that he'd been the first Elvis impersonator and had been working the strip in Vegas when The King came to town and had given him some moves that helped refine his act.

"So, anyway, these Elvis slingers, what I called 'em, were looking to put me down. Fastest on the draw replaced by fastest in the hips. What much of America doesn't realize is that the Elvis impersonators of today are doing impressions of *me*, not Him. For twenty years I was the man. Nobody could touch me, except The King himself, and more than once he did."

"How so," urged Tarleton.

"He'd reach down from heaven and do things for me."

"Like what, straighten your tie?" asked Randal, as Tarleton glared.

"Not little things, big things."

"Once I had gotten laryngitis overnight. I was on a double bill with the Frog Ladies of Avalon and went swimming with them after the show. Next morning, I couldn't talk. I had no voice at all."

"So, you had a frog in your throat," encouraged Randal, but his tone was wrong. As Tarleton seethed, Mabler leaned close and glared at the boy, pencil thin shafts of light from the Venetian blinds glinting in his pompadour.

"Make fun if you want, but I tell you this. I prayed for help and that night I sang better than I ever had, but it wasn't *my* voice, it was the voice of Elvis himself!" Mabler paced, as though the memories were too vibrant to take sitting down.

"A while back you said the counseling wasn't having the desired effect," said Tarleton, "what did you do?"

"Well, that was the point where I realized my approach was all wrong."

"How's that?"

"Elvis wouldn't have done it that way. I think he'd a talked to somebody close to him, like his wife. But I wasn't married at the time, so I went to my manager."

"The famed Sapphire Sal?"

"None other, she—"

"Excuse me," said Randal, "but she's one of my mom's heroes." Mabler stopped pacing and eyeballed the kid.

"It was the World Championship really made her famous, the spark that lit up Ladies Wrestling big time. She retired at the top, opened a wrestling school, and that's what got her into the talent market."

"Well, my mom had a poster of her pinning Dara Dare. Was she a pretty good manager?"

"A-number one. She got me on a step program until I walked clear of peanut butter paralysis."

"What's she doing now?" Tarleton relaxed as Randal seemed to go with the flow.

"Last I heard she was head of promotion for the Psychic Network telethon that was raising money for the House of Representatives' mosh pit."

"It just goes to show you," said Randal, beaming proudly, "that short people have more spunk."

"Son, she's not short, she's a midget. Make no mistake." Tarleton steered the conversation back to Mabler's disappearance.

"Well, I'd gotten married, and Betty wasn't cut out for the road. Besides, her *Priscilla* had problems from the get-go. But by then, the end was near." He stood looking out the living room window, and into the past.

"Was this about the time of the bowling alley incident?" asked Tarleton.

"That was pretty near it for us, a couple more shows. Listen guys, I need to go pick up my wife."

Tarleton steered Randal toward the door. "Mr. Mabler, I thank you for your time and your generosity. It's quite a story."

"Ramseur, my time won't mean a thing if they find me out. We've got it pretty nice here," he gestured, taking in a sweep the red dirt yard.

They drove back into Round Wilson for lunch. Tarleton sniffed the air and pulled to the curb at Claude's Bar BQ, a bookend storefront sandwiched between a piece goods shop and a furniture store. "You like Barbeque," he stated, as Randal trailed taking in the deep blue sky against the sheer green slopes. Behind them a girl rode her bike up the street, a smile planted in her brown face.

~ ~ ~

Button parked her bike behind the counter and chatted with her co-worker who tended to be quiet. Button thought it was cool that she didn't have a car, that her husband always dropped her and picked her up. Sure enough, the truck with the tinted windows pulled up out front, and Mrs. Betty Mabler rode off down the street toward home.

Button made the rounds with the feather duster that she'd decided was *not* made of bird feathers. There'll be no dead animals here, even if birds aren't animals. It's a spirit with a heart and a voice, and birds sing ancient prayers and chant the mysteries of life. Jam and others had shown her many times how to be respectful of the creatures we live amongst; it's not the other way around, they'd said. As she dusted the planar surfaces of a milky quartz crystal, she lost herself in thoughts of nature's ever-changing bounty.

4

A crow-fly mile to the west and standing over a stream, two men also talked change. From a distance they resembled an O and I: the rotund man was the Reverend August Tarbush of the Riley County Freewill Baptist Church. The other man, more lean than thin, was named Harlan Riggs, a real estate developer and recent transplant.

"Members of my congregation believe there may be ore in these hills."

"I doubt there's ore anywhere up here," said Riggs.

"A shepherd, sir, is not in the business of doubting his flock."

"We can take some samples, get them analyzed, see what we have, but in the long run it may not be worth it."

"Not worth it? Why, this entire end of the valley could be one huge mine …" and the Reverend's thoughts trailed in the train of untold sums.

"Why, we could have castles in the Bahamas, summer homes on the Cote de Azur, why hell fire, we could buy us a whole new church. Something I've been keening on for some time. Why, I would use this land here to finance the New Millennium University, a Bible college sir, the best in the land." Riggs regarded him then, a sleepwalking pragmatist.

"Reverend, once you get to mining here there won't be any place left to build so much as an outhouse," and Tarbush appraised him with a growing frown.

"You don't sink a shaft to get the kind of minerals you'd find around here, if they're here at all. No, you ever heard of strip mining?"

"Can't say as I have," hedged the Reverend, resisting the intrusion into his dream.

"Strip mining is cheaper and safer in the long run, but you turn the land into a moonscape." Tarbush glanced up at the crescent slice of white light.

"Oh, you'd make a pile alright, but you'd wreck all this," said Riggs, scanning mile upon mile of green in the deep blue haze and splattered with autumn's ochre.

"Don't tell me you're a tree hugger," said Tarbush.

"It's like this, you build on top of the earth, you got unlimited growth potential; you build down inside it, all you got is limit. There's only so much you can get, and that's it. What I see up here is development: chalets around a shopping mall.

The Reverend listened as Riggs went on, but he still clung to the idea of the mine and the blasting that would take that commune from the rear and drive them out like lepers. He combed his wispy hair— the wind kept raking it down his face—and imagined the power he'd derive from informing the flock that he had finally conquered the devil worshippers in their midst, that they were now on a mission as God's chosen salvagers to vanquish all the forces of darkness etcetera and so on. Then he'd go after their store; that girl, and her little dog too!

"A Beemer parked in every driveway," the real estate man said, as Tarbush re-entered the conversation, the reverie tingling fingertips and his knees seemed to ring.

"There are waves of retirees filling these mountain communities. You look at the numbers and you'll see how the demographics are changing this part of the South. I say it's time to act. Jumping on the bandwagon isn't enough. I say become that wagon. Let others jump on or fall off. What do you say to that, Rev?"

"Amen," was all he could think of as they walked back up the slope.

Tarbush sat a while in his Cadillac after Riggs departed, looking at the hills, one of which contained that infernal center for pagan studies. I'll get rid of those hippies once and for all. It's been what, twenty-five, thirty, too many years. He looked at himself in the rearview mirror: his doughy cheeks were tinted from the climb, and he tried again to square his thimble jaw that ever seemed to point like a bird dog. 'I never liked this jaw. Was it better before? Well, it was the only choice.' He started the engine. 'It could have been me up there, but I'm a lot smarter, and they'll see just how smart when I get this deal.'

~ ~ ~

Harlan Riggs scanned another file, the click of the mouse the only sound as he scrolled down the list of names crosschecked with their known aliases and highlighted one as he pondered the layers that concealed the man from the fugitive. All of his years at the Bureau had taught him that details, painstaking search, and patience were the keys to success, and the latter foremost. He unrolled a survey map of the county and looked it over. Of course, *success* now had a double meaning, provided he worked the Reverend into his corner. He believed a little more coaxing would do it, and he could dovetail the two projects into one. Now suppose one of those hippies really was their man, wouldn't a string of chalets peering over the ridgeline drive them to protest? He'd attempted various ways of getting on to their land to look them over, talk to them, but they'd shown no interest in real estate beyond their own, on which they spent most of their time. 'Well, this has the ear marks, could be it then, they're known to be environmentally active.' Again, he looked over the map: any run off, whether real or imagined would seep into their back yard and likely send them scurrying to the courthouse, 'the very place I aim to land one of them, anyway.'

For more than forty years the FBI had been looking for a bomber. In 1968 one Ralph Bannister had been a protégé of Jerry Rubin in the Youth International

Party (YIPEE!) and a magnetic speaker and motivational guru of the Left. His ability to draw folks in an induce them to act was legendary in the movement. Another one of his more popular specialties was his invention, manufacture, and demonstration of garbage bombs, harmless devices that sprayed rubbish and putrescent goo. According to the manifesto, the bombs were socio-politico-cultural-environmental statements that were designed to exemplify the absurd in their victims' policies, rules, or beliefs, and yet had been nothing more than guerilla theatre until one of them went off prematurely and claimed a life. Republican Senator Mack Snivekin was killed at a fundraising dinner when a ballistic acorn squash stuffed with rotten hamburger hit him square in the mouth. He'd choked to death in spite of a triple Heimlich bypass maneuver and a valiant, if not heroic, attempt by a house custodian inexpertly wielding the serpentine flex-hose attachment of a Hoover floor model. Ralph Bannister had gone underground as Rubin headed for Wall Street.

Oddly, at about that time the hippie commune had started, and the Bureau's tip that Bannister might be in the area was based on his eastern seaboard habitué and his signature use of organic vegetable devices, thus the hippies who'd decamped from New York to preach New Age farming in the hills near Ashville were an obvious target, regardless of how old the lead. 'Now,' thought Riggs, 'there's that other group, and they're no less insular and outlandish, but they're new here. I'll check them out, for sure, but none of them fits the profile.' He gazed into the Blue Ridge and contemplated a rosy future.

5

Button too was employed that afternoon in a form of contemplation as she worked to figure out the boy she'd come to know as Dingle, a moniker she came up with by the way he jiggled the door when he entered Blue Jay Way, oscillating the cowbells hung by Cody. They'd met at college and hung out together and once necked beneath a cliff face rumored to attract eagles. As he helped her arrange a display of tie-dyed doilies, Button played with what a life might be like as Mrs. Dingle but was interrupted by the cowbell and then Dingle was seen to bolt for the storeroom.

"Good afternoon," she trilled in Southern Belle-esque as the customer entered, not making eye contact as he strolled about the shop examining the merchandise, and then selected two packs of lavender incense.

"Haven't I seen you somewhere before?" smiled Button. "Why, you're the Reverend at the revival, are you not?"

"Well, y-y-yes," he said, jowls ruddling as she made change.

"I went there once because the music was sweet, but I didn't care much for the singing," she said with a wink and a curtsy. With a mumble he left the store, and she went in back and held Dingle's hands. "Now what was that all about?" she asked. He turned his face aside.

"What does the reverend, you know, he runs the Baptist chur—" she looked him full in the face. "He's your father? Reverend Tarbush is your father!" With a howling laugh she shoved him, and he knocked over a display. They bent to pick up spillage.

"When you said he was a writer, I wouldn't have guessed *sermons*," she said.

"Aw No! No way, you're selling *these* now?" he declared.

"Beats meat, and pure protein," she said, "micro-livestock is all the rage. Should have been here yesterday, we had a run of grasshoppers."

'I don't believe this!' he trembled. "You shouldn't, you, you, eat gnat larvae!"

"Well, the sign says it but that's what we sold yesterday. Poof, they were gone." She read his disbelief as curiosity: "The cult got them," she said.

He stared.

"You know, up on the hill, and it's like the third time. I can't imagine what, unless it's micro-gumbo every Tuesday."

"I never saw these here!" he sputtered. Of course not, she mused, with your eyes always on my bod.

"Well, we're mainly health food and organic grains, earth friendly stuff," she said.

"How can you be earth friendly and sell bugs? They're part of the food chain," he cried, "remove them and the whole thing crashes!" He fought to keep his voice level.

"I don't think you can *remove* them," she giggled, "I mean, there're gazillions of insects."

"What right do *you* have to kill them?" he said, a little too loudly.

"I haven't killed anything. What's your problem?"

"You traffic in death you're guilty as charged!" he cried, reeling off another slogan.

"You're not making sense. Here, try these, they're sugared."

"It's an abomination!"

"Caramel ants, get a grip," she said, as he reeled out the door, clutching the glossy evidence for a shady reunion, while she contemplated the Soap opera she'd scripted for the reverend and tallied the episodes. She had gone to a tent Revival to satisfy a curiosity, more dubious rather than drawn, but she had ducked the crowd to poke around the arena's backstage, pondering the consequences of some ill-defined delinquency, when he had approached her and stated flat out, he would do anything, anything at all to hold her in his arms. Like handling vipers, she thought, giggling, and told him out of the blue to kiss her boots. His willingness to please obliterated the mischievous tone of her command as he prostrated himself and she thrilled at the very idea: she'd tease him for pocket money and have a little fun in the bargain, and so far, he hadn't ceased to worship at her altar. And now Dingle, she thought, as petulant and needy as his dad but no hypocrite.

~ ~ ~

The Reverend Tarbush stormed into his house and slammed the door. "That bitch!" Then, aghast that his wife might be home, he stood still and listened to the ticking of the grandfather clock. Playing the coy salesgirl, teasing me, ME! She knew what I wanted, damn it, and she dangled me in that web of bugs! As he fumed, he imagined flushing the incense in the toilet, but then remembered flinging his purchase out the car window. Litter bug. He sank into an easy chair grateful that his children weren't there, and let his mind ramble and in so doing gazed at the cross formed by the window mullions as throngs of hysterical, half-naked people streamed to him, genuflecting at the foot of his throne as he raised a gauntlet—

"Augie, are you there?" shrilled his wife's nasal soprano, shattering the reverie, his benediction was gone in a blink as he beheld her two hundred pounds of fluorescent pink and ochre sundress and cookie dough face, mascara running under the freight of a towering blond beehive. "Look what I've found!" she said, "matching dachshund bookends!"

"They're just too dear," he mumbled, rubbing his eyes, and she embraced him.

6

Tarleton Ramseur entered his office at the Mountain News to find Randal awaiting him. He ignored the boy as he put away his things and settled into his chair. Well, something's afoot, that much is clear, but we'll just wait him out. As Randal's mentor, Ramseur had settled on a course of patience and low-key guidance that he intended to parallel to his semi-retirement and part-time status. As for instruction, the kid seemed to be a natural born journalist the way he bumped into stories. Ramseur checked his email and bided his time, but the silence did him in.

"Go ahead and spit it out," he said, leaning back and lacing his hands behind his head.

"Mr. Ramseur, something terrible has happened. I don't know how to say it."

"Then just say it." They sat for a while and looked at each other.

"I lost it," said Randal, at last.

"Lost what?"

"I don't know where it went, but it's gone."

"What is?"

"I've looked everywhere, but I can't find it."

"Find what?" asked Tarleton, as he followed the bouncing ball.

"Only place I haven't looked is home."

"Well, that may be where it is," suggested the big man.

"Except that I didn't take it home."

"Listen son, I can't help you if I don't know how to begin."

"Well, you're really going to kill me," said Randal, with a nervous chuckle.

"You're right. I *am* going to kill you if you don't tell me what we're talking about."

"And you're gonna kill me when I do," said Randal.

"Then what do you have to lose?" reasoned Tarleton.

"I'm really sorry, Mr. Ramseur, but I left the Courier on my desk, and now it's gone."

"The Mabler interview?" said Tarleton, his brows rising which seemed to pull the rest of him out of his chair. Randal's head bobbed like that of a toy dog.

"Son, you must learn to protect your source, always. It's the single most important thing to remember. Hey, heads up. We'll look for it," he said, as he laid his arm on Randal's shoulder.

In the early days of Randal's apprenticeship, the Ramseurs has given him a furnished room in their Raleigh home when the kid's widowed mother had leased the Poe residence and relocated to Colorado. Later, when the Ramseurs bought a mountain home in which to retire, Tarleton had instead taken a post with the Asheville Mountain News and brought Randal along with him, settling the kid in the carriage house. That evening they searched it without success.

"Protect a source like she's your sister, your wife, someone you love dearly and hold in the highest regard," said Tarleton, as he paced, a bottle of Rolling Rock in hand. "It is rule number one. If you don't establish that rule early on, you will have no story but ultimately no career."

"And we don't have a story now," lamented Randal.

"*You* don't have a story, son. The only hope is that the tape wasn't taken off your desk, although I suspect it was. That newsroom is full of sharks."

Randal jumped to his feet. "Stolen?"

"Probably, you're the new kid on the block, and that would be reason enough. Some of them resent the easy way you got in. I should have foreseen that."

"Mr. Madison doesn't even want me in there. He keeps changing my desk. It's not right."

"I'm sorry to hear it," said Tarleton, without reiterating that he and Poke Madison went way back. "But you don't *need* to be in there, I've said that before."

"I want to be a team player," said Randal.

"Son, your laptop is *networked* to the paper. You could work on the moon."

"What I'm going to do then is help him out," said Randal.

"Just sit tight. If there's no fallout, you can assume it was lost on the street somewhere."

"What do you mean by fallout?"

Tarleton eyed him. "Let's just hope we don't see your story under someone else's byline."

But what happened was far worse. That evening after the newscast ended, somewhere between weather and sports, Tarleton turned off the TV, and hung his head.

"Well, they certainly didn't dilly-dally," said his wife, Carolotta, as she rubbed his neck.

"I gave the boy too much free reign, cut him too much slack. Well, I'll call Mr. Mabler and give him the bad news. That's the least I can do, and perhaps I can salvage a tad of dignity from this." But before he had moved, the phone rang. Tarelton's face grew long as he listened, tried to squeeze in explanations and apology, and then stood looking at the phone in his hand.

"Not the boss," said Carolotta, as her husband returned to the couch.

"No, it was Mabler, gave me the third degree and then some. He should have given me more. I couldn't get a word in edgewise, though, about Randal's determination to salve the wound."

"Well, I know a short-term solution for pain," said Carolotta, "Come here."

~ ~ ~

Delray Mabler slinked like a shadow through the door of Blue Jay Way, closed it, and lowered the rice-paper blind.

"Hey there, Del, what's shakin?" said the girl behind the counter. "She's down to the Tastee Freeze getting us some sodas."

Mabler paced until his wife entered the store, and in the back hall they huddled in whispers that grew in pitch and finally the clerk excused herself and took her Nehi out the door.

"Damnit, Del! I told you this would happen! I warned you, didn't I?"

"Honey, I—"

"You weren't thinking about me, or about Ray. Oh no, you—that'd be too much to ask," and with that she broke down.

"Baby, I know it's bad, but look, we'll work it out. We—"

"No!" She pummeled him, her hands drumming his chest. "No, no, no! No more running! I want a home! I had one too! What now, more motels?" She turned away and he reached to console her with a handkerchief, but she slapped it away. He thought he saw a way clear for now. They'd had a similar fight before Ramseur's interview, and he'd been able to calm the waters by crooning a few bars of *Love Me Tender.*

As Mabler began to sing his wife dried her eyes but then turned without warning and clouted him, raking the wig from his head where it sailed it into the gemstone tray, marshaling lapis lazuli into the tourmaline.

"You ruined our life Del! Ruined it! We had it right, we finally had it right, and you threw it away!"

"Damn it, I was betrayed! That lard ass reporter sold me out, he—"

"I'm taking Ray. We're going to mother's, Del. Don't call. Don't make any attempt to—"

"You can't! We'll stick it out, the three of us!" She hugged him then, and whispered something, and he sagged. As Mrs. Mabler left the store, the clerk came back in, set her soda on the counter and stopped dead. She'd seen him on the History Channel and now here he stood, wonderfully out of sync beneath a poster ad for the songs of the humpbacked whale. Mabler faced her, his expression misty as he retrieved his hairpiece and mustache and repositioned them.

"It's not what you think," he said. She gawked at him a while more before Delray felt his knees give at the thought of that house of cards tumbling once again as he embarked on 'the explanation.' But for once, he didn't finish it.

"I see," she said, and winked. Delray looked her over: she wore her brown hair braided and stuck through with feathers and beads, a safety pin pierced through one cheek, mini-handcuff earrings dangled, and a paper-thin sundress offset by embossed black combat boots. He'd seen her a dozen times and never really noticed.

"I'm Sandalwood, I work with your wife," she reminded him. "You need a place of refuge, a hide-out." It wasn't a question.

"How did you know?" He leaned over to retrieve the wig.

"Del or El or whoever you are, I'd love to do your chart. I read auras and chakras, and right now your energy fields are down."

A customer came in and Mabler busied himself among the racks of New Age CDs, feigning an interest in Yanni until she spoke to him again.

"I know a place nearby," she said. "My boyfriend lives there. You ever heard of the Mystic Knights of Moonstone Light?"

"Can't say I have."

"It's like a secret society. You'd be safe there, I know it. Tell you what, you grab your stuff and I'll make the arrangements. Come back in an hour?" and she winked at him again as she picked up the phone, but Mabler used it first.

At home, he stormed around the trailer like a manic porter. Record albums and mementos tossed into pillowcases and clothing and hairpieces flung, all, that is, except the white leather suit, which he folded with the reverence of the national flag. As he laced his blue suede shoes and headed out the door, he vowed to reunite his family at any cost.

7

At the outset the building had been called the Center for Celestial Studies and for which the hippies had cleared a knob to the west of Rainbow Run, built the structure, and put in a road. But astrology was a hard sell, and the view, while spectacular, was no greater than many others. Prior to what Jam referred to as 'the Shangri La effect' took hold and saw an exodus of many ("goin' down that road feelin' bad") they composed the astrological charts of friends and visitors and spent many a stoned night beneath their timber framed dome.

Yawning above the hall was a forty-foot-wide rotunda of glass and steel, a modified version of the one invented by Buckminster Fuller a few miles down the road at Black Mountain College. It became the butt of jokes among locals. If they had known, the dome was intended to represent a zodiacal circle of 360 degrees, and if they had counted the mullion, they'd have found twelve segments, each with an arc of 30 degrees. If they had stopped laughing at this point, they would have discovered that the segments were called *houses*, each individually significant and ruled by its sign in the zodiac. But so long as it wasn't devil worship, then it didn't really matter. Longhairs build a barn to look at the sky, well, okay. Many others build a shed just to make liquor, and so acceptance was certain and tolerance true, like veins of gold in granite.

"Why a domed ceiling?" Jam had asked, as he stood beneath the arcing glass in the newly finished building.

"It's helios, man, and helios pulls everything and everyone, it gives life and is in charge for your heart, your eyes, and your sperm," said Amanda. "Also, in astrology the sign for the sun is a circle with a dot in the center, like a breast."

"I can dig it."

"The sun sign is like your basic sign and from that's determined your aura, you know, like if you're hip or not," she said, while above them Cody, observing from a perch on one of the exposed beams, sent smoke rings that descended like ethereal leis upon children chasing balloons.

They'd had an ongoing discussion on potential uses for the structure, and a favorite had been a concert hall. Sure, a gig here would be cool, but what band is gonna trek all the way out here and like, we're the only audience, instructed Cody. No, they'd use the space for what it had been designed for. It was out of this discussion, now only vaguely remembered so many years on, that had grown the sprout of turning a profit. In those days making money wasn't an issue, or better said, not making money was an issue worth defending against the homogenous and faceless corporate world they'd left behind.

"We just didn't accept that as a world view," explained Cody, as he and his daughter viewed the distant dome, its cupola a thimble looming above the tree line like a surreal teat.

"It was a time of alternative ideas and new perceptions, or at least we thought they were new. We sought a different definition of reality, a distinct approach to the one we'd been handed by our parents. We were expected to take the mantel of their reality and wear it, slip it on like a polyurethane sleeve."

"What was wrong about their reality?"

"They had, you know, like a world war that supposedly leveled everyone; it didn't, but that presumed commonality led to their complacency; everything was just too pat. Later, when the celestial study vibe didn't work out and we rented the space; it seemed we'd grown complacent too. Now we just collect the rent," said Cody.

"Reverend Tarbush wants to put his bible college up there," said Button.

"I know a better place he can put it," said Cody. "But you know, it may be several ridges away, a crow-fly mile, but it's still our land, and I don't want Bible thumpers howling hosannas in the laurel."

"Cody, he says he's gonna drive the heathen out of the valley, and I think he means us, not the Night Lights."

"Hah! Good one, that's what you call them? I like it. I don't know what they are beyond star-gazers like we were, and I don't really care, Button." A hawk soared past, wing tips tracing its path through the trees. "That's steady income, honey, and it's already helping put you through school."

~ ~ ~

Delray Mabler was seated beside a tow-headed young man who squinted every time he took his eyes off the road to look at him as the truck growled through the switchbacks. Mabler was sure they'd vault the guard rail and burn in a gully. "Watch your speed now!" yelled Mabler as the kid blew a pink bubble the size of his head that wobbled in the slipstream before he resumed his chewing and popping, gum cracking like a fighter's knuckles. On a dirt road cul-de-sac, they parked in front of a blockhouse and the kid ran inside. Mabler removed the hairpiece so as to wipe away sweat and then got out of the truck to survey his surroundings, a clearing ringed by mountain laurel thickets that held four log-built structures. The largest of them was capped by an arching dome. The compound was encircled and cross-hatched with galvanized chain link fence. He leaned against the truck and looked at the sky, stands of white pine against the blue like sentinels, their limbs interlocked high above in the crisp fall air. Behind him a voice rumbled: "Welcome, sir, right this way," but when he turned there was no one there. He hefted his bags and stepped into a dim hallway. Light glowed from behind an open door and as he stepped through it he encountered rows of smiling people clad in Kelly green and Mylar pajamas, silver rings the size of soup bowls dangling from their ears. They stared. He stared.

The room was bright with light from an expansive sunlit dome that arced overhead like a bubble, and Mabler stood in an amber shaft as though anointed by the sphere, and his lapel pin flashed. An adoring fan had designed the stud that read 99 9/10, but through the years as the glue and laminate and impersonator too had aged the numbers had slipped and now read 999/. As the stud twinkled, a choral gasp arose in unison: "It's the Anti-Elvis!" Mabler's instincts replaced his awe when in unison they bowed as one and he launched into *Love Me Tender* and at the far end of the room a man seated in a velvet butterfly chair perched on a dais beckoned to him.

"Dr. Argon Kyrkcops, sir, at your service. For you alone, I am Argon." Mabler beheld a heavier version of the Mr. Clean logo on the detergent his wife bought. Glowing beneath the shiny pate were eyes of smoky ice. Mabler bowed and was invited to sit.

"Your advent, sir, is prophesied in the Cydonian Scrolls, although I didn't expect you so soon," said Argon. Mabler nodded but held his tongue. His attendees seemed to know everything about him, as befit the King, but there hadn't been a single request for a song. He guessed they were on to him.

"It is also prophesied that your legions would be unknown to you, as witnessed upon your manifestation, a fulfillment of that prophecy, although further legions are due to throng." Mabler nodded sagely and stroked his chin in repose.

"It is my honor as Grand Sorcerer to uphold my duty to the Scrolls and reveal just who we are, not of the flesh, but of the mind."

Mabler spent the next hour at the head of a receiving line greeting his host's devotees who filed by in the altogether, *sans pajamas*, and while several voluptuous bodies took his breath away, many of them were frightful. It reminded him of a concert he'd given once at a California Toastmasters nudist camp. When at last it was over, his relief was momentary.

"The Mystic Knights of Moonstone Light was established five Julian years ago, but light years in the range of Aquarius; we are an educational and scientific organization; we have open membership but are non-profit; our mission statement is devoted to reverse regressive evolution through the spiritual revelations channeled by myself and by our High Priestess and Keeper of the Krystal, Mrs. Nungesser, whom you have just met."

Mabler had been horrified at the spectacle. It was bizarre enough to be introduced to a train of naked strangers, but with the aforementioned, he'd wanted to make a run for it. Before him loomed a half ton of lily-white and quivering flesh. She curtsied, presented a teaspoon, and bent it double by ogling. Stunned less by hypnotic trance than her gelatinous pontoons, his skin wanted to crawl off his bones.

"We also channel Samadhi trance energy through the chakra jewels of our kingdom selves with those of the Elohim, thus connecting the Atlanteans on Mercury with those who remain on earth," said Argon. "The Elohim, otherwise known as The Seven, will send a signal for us when our mission is completed, that we may join our brethren at the next level."

Holy shit, thought Mabler, I'm trapped in a remake of The Jetsons.

"Of course, the problem is in knowing which seven we're dealing with," said Argon.

"I don't follow you," replied Mabler, and his host fixed him with a puzzled look.

"As you know, there's a good Seven and an evil Seven, and that's where you come in."

"Why yes, of course! You'll excuse me, I was drifting," said Mabler. And he had been, for whoever he was supposed to be was someone who knew a great deal more than was comfortable, an imposition even for a veteran impersonator. That he was supposed to have insider knowledge on gods and planets and ETs made him squirm. He took a chance.

"How is it that this legion of the Mystic Knights came to be?"

"I'm glad you asked, but to be fair, I must begin with myself, if you'll so permit," said Argon, waving away the Mylar suited waif who'd brought them tea.

"I was once a college professor."

"No kidding," said Mabler, thinking, Mars Hill?

"Yes, Bob Smith University."

"That's down in Spartanburg, South Carolina, am I right?"

"You're thinking of Wallace Beaver," said Argon. "No, Bob Smith is at Pukie Corners; that's twelve miles south of Columbia."

"Yeah, okay, is it a Catholic school like Wallace Beaver?"

"Bob Smith is fundamentalist Protestant."

"That's like Baptists?" asked Mabler.

His host looked as though he'd farted protoplasm. "Sir," he intoned: "Baptists are . . . Bap— I'll put it this way, if religion could be compared to a pack of dogs, Baptists would be the poodles."

Mabler waited for further clarification, but his host swept onward.

"Helping out in the bookstore one day I checked in an order of Bibles. We moved more of them than Hallmark sells greeting cards. But when I unpacked the crates, I found that our order had gotten mixed up with another. Instead of sixty of the King James in tawny leatherette we had us two hundred pop top cans of Beanie Weenie."

"That's a heck of a tradeoff," offered Mabler, noting the misty eyes of his host.

"So, I drove it all up to Columbia. On the way back about dusk I saw strange lights off in the woods. I crossed a cattle guard into bottomland and the next thing I know I'm sitting in a stainless-steel vat of opaque Jell-O conversing with an eye the size of a truck tire."

"What did you talk about?" inquired Mabler. Having lived a tall tale, he was intrigued.

"We spoke about Atlantis, of all things. I didn't know squat about mythology, but what came out of me spilled like a millrace."

"So, this took place in a UFO?"

"I don't know, but we weren't in *Kansas* anymore. I was somehow transported to a vaulted place where many creatures were chanting a rhythm, like a mantra or an eerie refrain."

"I'd like to hear it if you can render up a version," said the phony son of Memphis.

"It was after this chanting, that's when I knew I was in a spaceship."

"What clued you in?"

"We rose above the tree line and higher, and in a blink, we were in deep space. We went to Mercury. I met God, was entrusted with the Scrolls, given my orders, and dismissed. I awoke in my car at a Roy Rogers on the New Jersey turnpike."

"Wow!" Mabler wanted to ask about God but didn't know how to frame the question.

"Or I should say a new man awoke there. I vaguely recalled my other life, as though it were some tale I'd read as a child."

"So, what did you do?"

"Well, the first thing was to order pancakes a la mode," said Argon, as he recalled an immense and radiant joy measured by an acre of orange booths.

"I meant, what about your job," said Mabler.

"The truly amazing thing," he softly confided, bringing their heads together over the tabletop, "was that I'd been gone almost two years."

"Get out of here! Two years?"

"No job. No wife, nothing, but I didn't know any of that until later. Like I said, I was a new man, a man with a mission."

"But how did you get started up again, was it on welfare?" asked Mabler.

"Well, the first thing I did was join the union. I became a member of the Teamsters Union of Clans, Cliques, and Cults Local #361 in Hackensack. Ahh, those were the days." Mabler pinched himself to check reality and to stay awake as his host droned his tale.

He took a job editing ad copy and writing stories that came to him in a trance state in which he didn't recall writing the tales. A supervisor's friend of a friend had gotten him an interview with a magazine publisher and soon after he was churning out reams of fantasy and sci-fi material. For every new magazine that accepted a story he supplied a nom de plume. And that fit well with his new life and identity. He was redefining himself with every plot, every story. For *Boy's Life*, he became Herbert Barnswallow. For *Light Years*, he was Sammy Sunaru, and for *Argosy*, Granger Nickelson.

It was his editor at *Light Years* that suggested his current name. A story about a radioactive cowherd had been rejected twice before the relative merit of the tale had been discussed, of which there was little. 'You're full of gas,' the editor had stated, 'you're like the argon in these light bulbs. I don't care how you change it, but the only cows that sell are in the supermarket.' When he first pronounced *Argon*, the fanciful surname loaded into his brain like a cartridge, and he then added the title of Ph.D. so he could wear a beret with conviction.

But not all of his writing had been fiction, as he had addressed the space time continuum, trance states, and UFO theory. As to the latter, the paradigm held that UFOs were primarily based on the moon in cavernous parking decks and used by aliens on time-share with earth as their laboratory. Mabler was startled by the poke in his side.

"That theory was mere hypothesis, but mine was by divination," said Argon. Mabler wasn't sure he knew the difference, but he was too preoccupied with stifling yawns to inquire.

"I got mine from the horse's mouth, and his teeth were good, yessiree, very good indeed! What's really happening, as you know, is that the galaxy is a vast race course. The planet, Amgems Neutron 3 on one end, and Earth on the other are the pylons, and black holes are exit ramps to the pit stops. One of those is located near Mercury and we believe it to be less a gas-and-go than the winners circle and grandstand review! And the reason the black holes are expanding is that every year there are more racers, attested to by increased earthly sightings."

"And the ones we see are what, dawdling?" asked Mabler, too tired now to play the game.

"In a sense, yes: while rounding the pylons some of them gyro through the Van Allen belts as though they're getting dosed, like a high for them, while others drop down into our atmosphere to see what's cooking."

"Gee, if you owned a headache powder company, think of the mileage you'd get out of your logo on the quarter panel of a flying saucer," said Mabler.

Argon frowned as though he'd noticed a dimple for the first time and strode from the room.

Mabler sat until he was informed that the doctor had retired. Before being shown to his room, he stopped by the library and browsed the shelves, finally selecting a dog-eared paperback set of *The Voices of Ubu Wilbur*, the multivolume biography of Edgar Cayce's renowned talking Schnauzer. While signing for the books he noticed that Argon had checked out twelve volumes of the works of Kilgore Trout: Interesting, he thought.

8

"That's very interesting, indeed, another bank job," said Harlan Riggs. Replacing the phone, he sat and steepled his fingers as he ran the gamut of what he knew so far, then poured a cup of coffee and stared across the valley as he drank it: Might be time to let the sheriff in on my little secret now that I've got *two* crooks to catch. This cover of real estate developer isn't panning out like I thought it would. He stepped outside and crunched to his truck. What was it about this particular spot that attracted two fugitives? He pondered the issue as he drove and as the pale sun winked through the crimson canopy behind the Farmers Market.

Riggs handed out questionnaires amid sizable piles of produce. It asked: *As development grows and land prices rise, how do you see your tax dollars at work?* It was a step in his good-developer approach, one that also aimed to include an environmental impact statement. He felt the campaigner's urge to press the flesh, and spied an aging hippie loading bushel baskets in a rust bucket pick- up.

"Mornin," he said with a smile. Cody paused in his loading to squint. Riggs thought, the man's got enough hair for three people, and flashed scenes from his past like foot chases with draft dodgers and enduring scratchy wigs and patchy rhetoric at anti-war rallies.

"What can I do for ya?" The ex-peacenik hound discovered a leathery hand.

"Harlan Riggs," he said.

"Name's Cody."

"Yeah, I've seen you around, and I've been meaning to say hello. I'm new here."

Jam rounded the corner with an armload of packing crates, set them in the truck bed, and went for another load. Riggs waved the questionnaire.

"It's about assuring the community that Emerald Forest Development Corporation is user friendly."

"Hmm. Seems that forest and development is oxymoronic. Between them yawns a graceless lacuna. You can't have both," said Cody.

"Well, you can if you do it right. See, I too am a product of the sixties when we learned how to husband the earth, not destroy it." Cody let that slide. The guy didn't look sixties, but then, few did these days. He knew himself as a holdout, but this guy just didn't *feel* groovy.

"These mountains are filling up with retirees, many from our generation," said Riggs. "They're the ones that we have in mind."

"Retirees," said Cody.

"Say, since we're reminiscing, were you ever in Philly? They had a pretty cool scene back around sixty-eight, nine." Riggs sprawled back against the truck like a brother as Jam returned.

"Pumpkins are hot, peppers are not," he said, addressing no one in particular, and walked off.

"Later," said Cody and caught up with his pal.

"Kind of a weird guy, ain't he?" They weaved through the

milling bib overalls to where Button was minding the sale.

"That ain't the question, my friend," smiled Jam as they stopped to admire a fat man hawking yams in a jazz of fall harvest. "The question is, what are pennies made of?"

~ ~ ~

Several miles away Randal pulled up in front of the Mabler place. The trailer sat in weeds and the only thing mobile about this home was the trash that drifted like tumbleweeds around its deflated tires, and he discovered that its abandoned look was earned. On a once taut clothesline creaking like a broken sonata, rotting pins suspended a faded wash, and from the door left clacking against its jamb came a sigh like a cosmic, *Oh Well.*

Randal rooted. He found two packets of Bicycle playing cards, both with the Jokers missing, four cross-stitch embroidered hankies initialed EP in a whorl of spun cotton, and a Studebaker hubcap loaded with a sundry collection of cufflinks. Randal thought of steerage. In the living room he noted patina-less ovals on the paneling where the gold records had hung, and a bottle of Lilac Brilliantine, its sole contents the stem of a plastic rose. With a sense that he'd missed this episode by a matter of minutes, he drove into the valley more determined than ever to set things straight.

As he entered the town, he followed the line of activity and thus discovered the market. The pulse of rural America, he thought, and reflected on his stint as T.R.A.S.H. quartermaster as he eyed a pyramid of acorn squash.

"Hey! Randal, am I right? It's great to see you again!"

"Button! Wow. Cool Beans! You get my email?"

As they loaded into each other, his heart ramped in his throat.

"What about *him*?" Cody asked Jam. "You get a whiff of heat?"

"I get a fog of passion," said Jam.

"More like a pea soup," said Cody, as Button made the introductions. Jam could see that Cody aced the guy and that Button was popping her buttons.

"How long you here for?" she said.

"You could stay at the farm for a while, but I've got to start school soon," she added.

"Well, that sounds more peaceful than a motel," said Randal.

"There's only one motel here anyway, and you may not survive. The place needs to be dredged."

They left Jam and Cody hunkered over beans and drove off. She aimed to give him the grand tour: the town, the store, and the futon in the back.

Later they languished outside on the store's fire sale pew, a bench for one and all. As the sun rolled toward tomorrow, he sought to recount the numerous orgasms while their gloss still embossed him, and anyway elation makes a lousy abacus. He went goo-goo recalling her silken looming ride as he parted the curtains; the arched swoop of her back; her breasts like olive teepees in the Land-O-Lakes, and she kind of resembled an Indian, a silken Modigliani-faced squaw panting for the wampum of his Kit and Caboodle Carson with a hot buffalo horn? Nah, a faux Elvis hunter who so far had luck and bad luck swapped like trading cards.

"I don't have a clue where he went," said Button, "but I'll ask around. I do know that his wife and son skedaddled for the homilies of Ponce de Leon Avenue in the Coca-Cola Capital."

"I have a sneaky feeling," said Randal," that he's still around here."

"Something I want you to see. We'll go tomorrow. As for Del, we can ask Gertrude the Bear. She knows everything."

Before Randal could ask, her tongue was wrestling his and the sun winking from a ridge-top kissed them both good night!

~ ~ ~

The following morning Button and Randal left the farmhouse early and climbed the hills behind it that rose up through pine into boulder strewn thickets of laurel to a berm that overlooked a single lane dirt road. They clambered down the embankment and again set off uphill; the going much easier then and they walked side by side, easy in their company and went on for quite a while until she stopped him at a point where the road angled and curved away, seen again at intervals below. A nearby slope was fringed with oak and topped by a large glass eye that stared at the heavens. On the way back, she told of her parents' escape from concrete that led to the building of a dome on their six hundred acres of idyll. They kissed in the road.

Back in the woods she pointed out another feature that to Randal looked no different than the surroundings until she stooped and rooted around, uncovering a cave.

"It's been smothered in leaves and stuff," she said.

"I thought you said it was bigger, or were you just excited?"

She hooted and squirmed in, calling back, "the mouth is small but just here it opens up."

Randal soon joined her like a hound sniffing the barbeque.

"Only question is, how far does it go?" she said, and a misguided kiss in the cinereal dark swiped his nape. They hauled in their gear; rope, water, and flashlights, essentials in the spelunking arts. Soon they were able to stand, and once their eyes adjusted to the halogen glare, Button showed Randal where she'd chalked surfaces in the tomb-like entrance and on down the passage that curved away and led them onward. Randal thought, if it looks like dirt and smells like dirt; it must be dirt.

As they explored further, headroom fissured into cathedrals and side passages dropped into vast cul-de-sac caverns.

"Turn off the lights," said Button, "let's see how dark it really is." Globules of yellow danced and faded to writhing bottle green shapes eaten by ink.

"This is dark," said Randal, as he sensed her musk.

"Ouch!"

"Try this," he said, "you like it?" Kneeling, their mouths groped and found each other, and belt buckles clinked and he rolled down her panties and nuzzled in to run his tongue along her moistened crease before she fed him inside her, and as they rocked, he sensed a primordial worm that bucked and shuddered and then exploded with a shriek. They lay together, Button drifting in steams of surreal light as their breathing subsided.

Resuming their trek, they continued upward but the cave just seemed endless and the chalk was running to stubs. They sat on a rock, shared an apple and a fruit bar, and prepared to head back when Button grabbed him. "Shhhhh."

"Did you hear that?"

"Hear what," he said, feeling downright dumb for the remark.

"It sounded like a woman laughing, a faint echo."

"Well, they say hearing cranks up a notch or two when eyesight—"

"Shhhhh!" They sat awhile listening to their hearts and other twitches, creaks, and gurgles. Randal knew then how a fart might collapse the fundament in a mouse and elephant episode. Then they both heard it, faint but distinct. A distant soprano or a meadowlark one couldn't say, but it was there. Button recalled Native American tales of spirits and then flashed on her 'aunt' Ruth, Gertrude the Bear's caretaker and her animal camp; she claimed only kindred spirits came to her.

"Wow, there it is again," whispered Button, "like a creek gurgling with faerie chants." She'd asked Jam one day as he hoisted the rear of a Karman Gaia.

"Have you ever seen faerie in the woods?"

"You can't *see* them," he'd said, "You hear 'em. If you listen, the forest will speak. Thing is, folks launch into the so-called wilds jabbering like baboons in over drive." Randal and Button continued to sit like statues, but the voice failed to register again. Following the chalk, they dusted each other at the cave mouth and covered the entry in a thatch of hand raked twigs.

9

As the neophyte spelunkers were prowling in the cavern, Millicent Tarbush was working down a merry lane of her own. She drove through town and on out the other side in regal Corinthian leather, but before she reached Mountain Laurel Boulevard, Round Wilson's lone gateway to the Blue Ridge Parkway, she hooked the Caddy onto Plumley Plank Road and hauled ass.

The lone house that fronted this sad excuse for a State Road swallowed her dust as she turned down the rutted track and looked for the deer trail, marked by a burl that resembled the nose of a famed evangelist, at the end of which stood a cottage that leaned into towers of feral Mulberry.

Lou Ann's Jeep was parked nose out in choke cherries, and Millie gave the secret knock: shave and a haircut, one bit. Soon they were in each other's arms and stumbling through bra straps, pantyhose, and other troublesome elastic appendage impeding. Squawk radio APBs fractured their amorous wind from time to time, but time flowed onward to the tympani of it all. After, they shared a single glass of claret before a beeper stepped Lou Ann into her deputy pants.

"No rest for the weary," she commented, receiving a peck from Millie who then held up pantyhose like an auctioneer.

"See any holes?"

"Ah know only two kind, assholes and quarry holes, and Millie, yer in the latter."

Reaching for her girdle Millie felt charged up; L.A. as she called her gal was as witty as a Mockingbird, and she didn't relish changing the topic.

"Sweet, there's something worrying the Dickens out of me."

"Why, Millie dear," said Lou Ann, "we both know you're not a hand wringer, eh?"

"Well, you are right of course. Hug me. There, I feel better; it is just a silly dream anyway, but I keep having it again and again; and it is always the same! Wouldn't that pester you?"

"You tell it to me and I'll shoo it away."

"Well, I find myself suddenly at the kitchen sink, you know that yellow apron? And every time it is as though I just arrived, that is the strangest part."

"Well, go on now, you can spill it."

"I have been confused by wire fences! It is like an arabesque, and every time I cannot get out because, because I am watched by, by—oh it is just too silly—a giant green eye!" She sobbed in her lover's arms and thought then of simpler times, and of their earliest encounter.

They had met beneath an eviction notice on a battered antebellum house rumored to be a crack haven. But its limestone chimney and corbeled oriels was doted on by the Reverend as the area's prime location for a revival, for fire and brimstone oratory. The Sheriff also wanted control and once abridged with collection plate indulgence, enacted law. Millie had brought sack lunches so that the poor or unhappy evictees wouldn't leave on empty stomachs, but the only soul she encountered was Deputy Lou Ann Strayhorn, whittling her molars on a toothpick.

"We don't want any vagrants here." Millie wasn't aware that there *were* any vagrants in Round Wilson, and she idly wondered what a vagrant looked like.

"Wild animals might get in too, being summer," the deputy offered, a patrol tidbit. As they spoke on that vagrant-vacant and baking veranda, Millie found herself tumbling to the ardent spirals she'd fought in college. Her only other weakness was algebra to which she finally submitted, although a craven memory of argyle sweaters dogged her; but outside of 2x + 9y harassment, guilt had saved her from moral ruin, but not this time around the flagpole. She pined for delivery by her rotund Baptist hubby, but her heart went the other way.

After that porch chat, they'd met again at the Tasty Freeze and shared a booth! Millie recalled how she'd felt drunk and unable to remember much more of that day that saw them window shop at outlet stores and catch *On Golden Pond* in matinee. They exercised on weekends, but lately a spate of interruptions had dislodged fervor. She suspected her husband's weekly brimstone tirades melted her resolve as much as they aligned other congregants on the straight and narrow.

The two of them stood tumescent in the cottage door, threshold sinking, and Lou Ann said: "I'm thinkin' on another line of work." The implied elsewhere alarmed the preacher's wife and so she planted a wet one.

"If you must leave me, dignify it with a proper shove."

"Leave! I'm not going anywhere, Millie! What's got into you?"

"Another job, the valley has so little to—"

"*Here*, it's right here, and it's only part time. Listen to this, and I was going to tell you anyway, but when the Mablers moved out I took up the payments on their home and it's just two paychecks to Disneyland! I aim to be a landlord!"

"A charm, dear, and that is the job?"

"It's, no, well it is, but I mean maybe a new art school or something," said Lou Ann, climbing into the Cherokee.

"An art school? Here?" Millie couldn't fathom it, but was handed a card, and as her deputized paramour ripped track in a swirl of pine straw, the preacher's wife fingered an embossed script:

"Mystic Knights Inter-Dimensional Conservatory. What in the world?"

~ ~ ~

In similar terrain another conversation was wielded between two other close friends. Reverend August Tarbush was out hunting the hillocks with Harlan Riggs and with his backup organist, Sheriff Bob Robert Weston. The two locals had been buds since the bearded Tarbush had hitch-hiked into town and was promptly given a by-your-leave tour in a county cruiser to the eastern most bends of the jurisdiction. In those days the department had its hands full what with long hair hippies on ridge tops and moonshiners in bottoms.

But it was that very Sunday Bob Robert's eyes like to jump off his face when the same transient arose in the pulpit clad in holy vestments. After the service his stammered apologies were returned with a warm handshake, and before long they traded favors like a pair of card sharps. The only dent thus far in their friendship had come when the regular organist called in sick with the tremors and the two nearly came to blows when *A Mighty Fortress Is Our God* was sung to the only tune Weston knew, *Red River Valley.*

This day they were accompanied by a mutual acquaintance, Harlan Riggs, and together they stood askance a lofty hill. Steep wouldn't get it by a stretch, thought the reverend, but he felt ready in his L.L. Bean twenty-four pocket khaki vest and orange cap.

"You see at knob a granite," said Weston, indicating a boulder the size of a house.

"Behind it, she drops down to a saddle. We go opposite ways on around em air boulders, and we meet up in the saddle," said the Sheriff.

"This is the place where you got that big buck," said Tarbush.

"Saw two more but couldn't get a shot or a shit. Let's do er," and they started up, Weston heading *yonder* and the other two angling up to the right. Tarbush soon fell behind Riggs and puffed like a steam valve, pausing every yard or so and then shuffling on before he appraised the knob, and it didn't seem any closer; at last, he rested on a deadfall and listened for gunshot, yet a breeze rivaled his wheeze and then passed on as a jet working toward Bermuda whispered, and he worried. Was it always this quiet? He withdrew a hipflask from a cargo pocket and suckled. Gee, the second nip tasted better than the first, the third better than your average layman's salary will allow. Pocketing the flask, he arose but tripped on his rifle sling and tumbled ass over

Baltimore rolling like a stone that gathered moss all the way to bottom where he'd begun the assent, and where he sprawled, pine straw sticking out of him like a porcupine.

"Godammit," and his fluster was then punctuated by the boom of a rifle. That was a 30.06, he said to the air, one he believed to be inferior to his own, wherever it may be. As he gathered himself, he noted soot all over him; he had been blackened. Following another snoot of bourbon, he caught sight of his toupee on the downhill track, looking like road kill, and wobbled to check it out as Riggs approached; having observed the tumble he had come to offer assistance, and together they determined the Reverend's skid had scraped ground cover to reveal a track like rubber laid by Richard Petty, and as he knelt in seasoned charcoal; the idea hit: why didn't I see it before, it's perfect: I'll burn them off that ridge!

"You alright?" Riggs came up carrying both their rifles "Looks like an old fire." He scraped away duff with a boot, revealing more blackened soil.

"Indeed, perhaps a lightning strike. Find the flashpoint, we'd know," said Tarbush.

"No way of telling, but it was a while back, these trees here are pretty big," said Riggs.

"Must have burned like a fury," said Tarbush, as fantasy ran a video zephyr of flame marching over Rainbow Run. The two started back up as Weston's rifle boomed again; the Sheriff met his quota, and the Reverend soared in the carbon ecstasy of his maker.

~ ~ ~

Button was another one soaring that day as she rode her bike through drift clouds up trails cut eons before by the forest service and still maintained with duty clearage and water bars to channel runoff. She rode the switchbacks like a champion ascending through billowing fingers of mist that lay like imparted whispers in the trees. Downhill now leaning into the bike and the gears for all that worthy machinery could, and at a point where the trail took a vertical plunge she launched and rolled clear in pine straw as the bike slid sideways, rear wheel spinning. The remainder of the trail was pretty tame and moments later she emerged from the tree line and saw the plume of wood smoke.

Ruth Broadman met her on the limestone veranda beneath the crest of Mt. Gertrude. Her home had once housed a park headquarters until it was swallowed by Teddy Roosevelt's administration and sectioned into the Pisgah National Forest. Her husband, a Pinchot crony was posted there and the couple had put the place on the map. Mrs. Broadman was currently the Round Wilson librarian and also the Florence Nightingale of fauna. As an empirically and spiritually trained veterinarian, she coiffed the estranged, mended the lame, and sheltered those lost from dens and nests. Town folk quipped that Ruth became the librarian because she was the only one fierce enough to grace the post, but her laugh alone could shuck corn. One animal hunts its dinner and another one reads about it, she'd often said, don't tell me otherwise. Such had been the case with Button who considered herself a well-read mammal who had crossed the line.

"You came at a good time, dear," said Ruth. "I just returned from downhill."

"How is she? I haven't seen her for two weeks."

"That old bear," she said, crinkling wrinkles, referring to Round Wilson's eldest resident, Gertrude the Bear. When her shave tail husband was hacking shingles from white pine slabs and marking trail, a black bear cub wandered into camp and took up residence in the walnut grove the newlyweds called home. They adopted the wayward cub and fed it leaves and larvae chum until it fended for itself. The bear adopted a local celebrity which over time grew to include the general region, and ultimately Gertrude's Grove became a national attraction featured on Esso highway maps! A then-popular bumper sticker read: *I Ate Dinner with Gertrude the Bear.* The town librarian regularly ushered busloads of visiting middle school classrooms into the grove.

"I'm proud of you, that poetry award," said Ruth, and soon you're off again to college."

"I brought you a poem," said Button. "I hope you like it."

> The mountains sit in their lumps, as traffic
> hums   from distant roads and
> hummingbirds get drunk on sugar. This goes
> on. The mountains in their green and blue
> mystery sit in their lumps as we auction their
> stumps and bleed their streams and gouge
> their gorges beneath relentless skies.
> This goes on and on, and still we love our
> loves, pick our nits and candidates and stack
> our lumber in priceless piles, as though
> attempting to out-mountain the mountains.
> This too goes on and the mountains sitting
> in their lumps, all grandmotherly appointed
> with doilies and flowered dresses, obtain us
> in all that Time has to offer.

Ruth folded the sheet into an airplane and sailed it.

"Child, your soaring wisdom is ageless."

"Not like yours; there are things about mountains that I would like to know, but especially our very own mountain," said Button.

"You know more than you gather."

"No, I mean like, can a mountain talk, can its caverns sing or chant?" She pictured herself in the cave grappling with her lover, the probing journalist, and felt a little silly.

"It can for our neighbors, the Cherokee. Native American religion was both terrestrial and animalian, all imbued with supernatural meaning."

"So, it's possible." Button told of the singing cave.

"That is quite a tale indeed," said Ruth, rolling a cigarette.

"We thought it may have been water, you know, trickling."

"But then you heard it differently the second time, confirmed by your friend."

"Maybe it was the spirit of the mountain," Button said. Ruth smiled.

"Now, it may well have been. Fortunately, we have at our disposal reams of printed matter as well as digital outlay. Let me see."

Button fed the raccoons housed in slatted cages, and then found her bike and rode for glory down the highway, less slippery but doubly dangerous what with nodding RV pilots and lead-foot campers hauling trailers stuffed with gizmo, eager for the choice pop-up rental site with full hookups and a trusty spigot. She was coasting down the long grade to the junction when she eyed Deputy Strayhorn turn up the road to the space station, as she called the place, home of the Night Lights, and she up-shifted for pursuit. What else was there to do in a small town?

Button crested the rise and hauled up at the front door and just behind the ticking Jeep and scowled at the compound; there'd been no change to the shabby construction and of unfinished buildings from an earlier report to her dad. It wasn't the Shangri la as Cody and Amanda and others described, but slabs in razor wire. Ah, but was that an unlatched gate? Cloud rolled in as she eased it open and stepped inside memories of hunting Easter Eggs and when her bunny, Mr. Jiggs, got lost up here. She was flashing on the distant Cody rescue of the errant hare when through the swirling vapor she eyed the lanky Mr. Mabler in the buff and wrapped in the arms of a Rubenesque woman, supine on a settee. She thought of a marshmallow on a toothpick. Soon they were bouncing the springs, a caveat to investors in the lounge-a-matic, a chair for all seasons. The clouds grew thick and the air chilled and the spying girl pondered the layers of sub-cutaneous birthday suits. For a better view she clambered up a pine in a fireman's crawl where she viewed the disrobed dame marching in place and belting out a martial tune as Mr. Mabler unfolded from the divan and raced for a door. Something about the woman seemed familiar, and Button stood on the pedals all of the way home, too puzzled to sit.

10

Delray Mabler huddled in a sheet to regain his composure, re-inflate his lungs, and review. Draped in a bath towel he had taken his soiled clothes to the Inter-Dimensional Laundromat whereupon the immense Mrs. Nungesser, retrieving a bundle of teddies, had cornered him between a purring dryer and the soap rack. How they ended up outdoors he didn't know, but he was certain that his love for his wife was sound and not the figment of an elephantine replacement. Winding the bed sheet around him, he scouted the hall before he scooted to the laundry and by the time he returned he'd not only gained his duds but the insight of the laundress, a pale waif in a poodle cut and clogs, that there wasn't much for him to do until "the day."

So far, he'd been unable to glean much about what this day meant or why it was esteemed, other than snippets about the earth mother, or maybe mother earth. It was okay by him. When the time came, he'd claim amnesia and duck the scene, given that he was professionally adept at disappearing from groupies and eluding the craven masses. Until then, he would simply kick back and read. He'd finished the Ubu Wilber and was now into the second book of Kilgore Trout's trilogy, *At Pluto, Hang a Louie.*

At the dog-ear he began to read about how the hero, an intrepid time traveler, had made a black hole in one on the back nine of the Andromeda galaxy . . . but he couldn't concentrate and soon recognized the house of post-coital bliss, and as he crossed the threshold and entered the foyer, he couldn't muster an ounce of revulsion over his seduction by a bovine mademoiselle who bent spoons for a living. He went for a stroll and as he turned toward the cafeteria in a cornbread trance, he ran into Dr. Argon, who bowed.

"I was just looking for you. I'd like you to join me for lunch."

"Funny you should ask," said Mabler.

"Come along, we can order from my office."

"BLT's?"

"You want it, we got it." Mabler arranged himself in the chair beside the desk as his host made the call.

"Tell me, just who *is* Mrs. Nungesser?"

"In this world, she is its premiere channeler and clairvoyant. Don't think her odd for certain nuances. She's often to be found conversing deeply with those on the other side," said Argon.

"Well, yes, I sensed that. But why is she naked?"

"She prefers the sheer nightie, but either way, clothing interferes with the alpha particles. Synthetic fibers act like a Van Allen Belt around her body."

"I see," said Mabler, utterly in the dark.

"She could try cotton."

"Ah, here we are," said Argon, answering a knock on the door. When the tray revealed a BLT on rye, Mabler winced. But when he peeked underneath and saw mustard his eyes went funny. I should have caught it, he thought. No true southerner calls this *lunch.* Across the desk he surveyed the stuffed face of his host and apprehended a Yankee. Was that why they all behaved so oddly? He'd known many and didn't hold grudges, but you had to admit they didn't always have both feet on the floor. He sighed and took a bite. As he munched the culinary sacrilege it dawned on him that the colossal clairvoyant could see through his guise.

"I have taken note of your healthy appetite for reading," said Argon.

Was this another feeler, a test question? Mabler wasn't sure of what his host was looking for, a herald, a harbinger.

"I enjoy the folly of it all, the total lack of perspicacity in the human rant," he said, and Argon regarded him through steepled fingers.

"You don't find it educational?"

"Oh, certainly, one can always learn a tidbit here, a universe there. Writing, I think, must lead," said Mabler.

"Yes! Yes, I agree totally," said Argon, whose glowing dome indicated an immediate weather break. He opened a drawer and extracted a hefty notebook and slid it across the desk.

"Volume I of my magnum opus: it is yet in progress. I'd be honored if you'd peruse it, let me know what you think." Before Mabler could respond, his host admitted a young woman.

"Excuse me, Q, but the intercom system is down and there's a message for you."

"Thank you, Lou Ann," said Argon. As she turned to leave, she caught sight of Mabler and stopped. He smiled and winked.

"Is there anything else, Lou Ann?" asked Argon.

"No Q," and as she left the room, she took in another glimpse of the King.

Lou Ann Strayhorn, Riley County deputy sheriff and newly hired part-time receptionist at the Mystic Knights Inter-Dimensional Conservatory left work that day abuzz. She was tempted to call the Sheriff but saw that this was too big a thing for him. She sensed the reason he'd encouraged her to take the new job was to get the low down on what went on there. Besides, she reasoned, I might could work this to my benefit. I'll tell you know who when I see her Friday week, but in the meantime a little investigation wouldn't hurt, starting with this. Round Wilson didn't have a bookstore and she wanted to check out that new Elvis biography, so she pointed the Jeep east and hit the road. She crawled along behind an ancient VW and when at last she passed, saw Button Springfield at the wheel and a boy she didn't know.

~ ~ ~

Randal felt like he was riding in a time machine, as indeed he was. They didn't make them like this anymore, and he recalled his father's disdain for models older than showroom. But he liked this wheeled metal teardrop.

Arriving at the campus they wove the freshmen melee where milling knots suggested semaphore drill and parental porters decamped of steamer trunks. Button spoke of her first two years and Randal reflected on how his denial of admission enrolled him instead in the school of hard knocks. But luck and savvy had secured him a good job and until now he hadn't been near a college, so he couldn't miss what he didn't know, he said, and laid a duffel on the pile. She gave him the grand tour, three rooms, a backyard gully choked with kudzu, and finally her garden in the vale where he groused among her buttons. Then they loped off for tofu burgers; Randal's instant veggie conversion a testament to her healthy loins

~ ~ ~

Elsewhere on campus Jensen Tarbush (known to our lively heroine as Dingle) was reading up on what he'd missed during the summer break: the newsletters chock-a-block with green snippets from the news services, as well as ongoing platforms, and he perused the plight of the marbled brown grouper before burying his nose in a piece that chronicled the dwindling numbers and habitat of the Moravian Spoon-billed Tit Licker. The problem seemed too expansive and he fell into a funk then and rambled through a range and clutter of perspectives. Like elephants: Okay, ivory is not worth dying for. Blow out the brains of pachyderm to hawk the tusks on the black market. So, it's a bad scene but not *my* scene. It's just way, way too big. No, I'll make a name for myself in a field so far ignored. Can't believe they don't see it, but they don't see it because its size is inglorious. He pulled up the data he had transferred to a spreadsheet before the summer break and in the glow of the monitor he again grasped that the font of his passion and the truest salvation of the planet lay in the smallest creatures of the bio-sphere. They were right. They'd seen right through me.

The previous semester he had checked out a nascent off-shoot group because the campus Animal Rights chapter was overcrowded, each section teeming with the eager and the loitering uncertain. For example, Laboratory Animals had a roster of nine, The Pound (Shelter) had five, and the Strays and Road-kill roster showed four and a half, given as they'd added the secretary's rug rat. Jensen wanted to shine in the movement, to stand out in the field, as it were, and not be swallowed up or left to rot in the contamination of anonymity. But an additional group, recently formed, was drumming for campus recruits, and though in its infancy, it was attracting attention. Although an initial spark drew him, he dawdled like a geek at a fashion show until he'd listened to the point-counter point of a student debate.

"Insects?"

"BZZZZZ!"

"No way. Like a mosquito is just—"

"A life! It deserves to live, too!"

"Not if it wants to suck my blood."

"That's how it eats, nourishes its young." Jensen sat rapt. They really had a way of opening it right up under your nose, forcing you to peer inside.

"The mosquito must give birth. Let us not escape that fact."

"Ho, born in blood? How lovely," said a spiky blond in a pink leather mini. "What about flies, huh? You know where *they're* born."

"It doesn't matter. What right do you have to end their lives?" The blond stalked off prattling. Jensen took her place at crowd's edge, and his eyes went misty when he heard that each and every species is a masterpiece of God's benevolent creation. None must be killed. All must live; to uphold a life is to make it sacred. As the gathering dispersed Jensen pinned on the button and admired its sheen, proud that he'd taken the plunge to become the campus chapter president of *Parasites Rights.*

Now back among the brethren and ready to shine, Jensen made notes as he massaged assumed love wounds. Though his friendship with Ms. Springfield was over, he didn't feel too badly about it all because his lust and infatuation with her had been abandoned in the cradle of *The Shove That Scattered the Larvae.* She was a death merchant, and he would shut her down, or she and her clients would have to pay.

Book Two

E Pluribus Elvis

Randal read the article a second time while trying to find his words and a sense that he'd actually written the piece that had his name on it but soon gave up and chewed his lip, instead of his liver. The demotion hurt, even though it was only temporary. The Police Blotter, other than a pod for interns, was the dumping ground for those who didn't follow the rules. Okay, might as well get on with it. He dialed the number to verify his appointment to interview a bank robber. As he drove, he noted the quilted overcast and thought it was perfect jail weather, confirmed by the gray industrial interior of the building.

Harvey Welch was ushered in and sat with clinking chains. He was hatchet faced and about Randal's age. The drooping lids gave away a boredom bound by institutional tedium.

"Hi, Harvey Welch, I'm Randal Poe."

"Who gives a shit."

"Well, you might when we light up the town with your name."

"Yeah? How you gonna do that?"

"I'll compare you to Jesse James and the like and make you into a folk hero."

"So, what's in it for you," said Welch.

"I want people to see what's real, to feel it. Yours is a true adventure story. Publicity never hurt anybody and might even help when your trial comes up. Besides, I'm the only outlet you've got." Welch sat hunched in his county orange duds and stared at nothing before he nodded a dozen times. Randal imagined the bouncing ball of the thought process but kept his council.

"All right, I'll give it to you in sections. Each section I need a carton of Marlboro and some mags, you pick them. But they won't allow some in here, seen a screw confiscate *Jugs*."

"Okay," said Randal, "no problem. So, how did you come to that bank, I mean, can you give me some background that will lead us there?"

"Background, oh well, that's a long one. Well, ah, I guess it started when I joined the BA in Idaho. You heard a them."

Welch lit a cigarette and Randal smoked second hand.

"Do you mean the AB?"

"We're an offshoot from them, had a falling out, come that close to a shootout. We took off east then and got us our own compound and a web page too. You can check it out at Beige Aryans dot org."

"Clue me in on that," said Randal.

"Well, Butch, that's our commander, he said we all pink on the inside and because of it want nobody truly white, said it was bullshit and a big lie and beige was more accurate. You can see how right he is." Randal pondered the double entendre while nodding his consent. Welch lit another one and Randal pictured pink lungs gone black in an ooze of goo.

"So anyway, we had a jamboree and invited everybody that wasn't already linked to the AB and had us a party where a lot of shit got worked out. We had biker gangs, single bikers, lone wolves, and bikers without bikes. Shoot, eight of 'em showed up in a Subaru—"

"Weren't the Pyrates, were they?" said Randal.

"Hell yeah, you *know* them?

"Wally Bugg and me go way back," said Randal, noting the approach of the guard.

"Well, I'll be a son-of-a-bitch! You get me the cigarettes and we'll have us a set to." Upon leaving the cell block Randal saw a man he thought he recognized. After speaking with the deputy who liaised with the media, he learned that real estate in Riley County had the interest of the Justice Department, but that in itself didn't explain the presence of Harlan Riggs.

~ ~ ~

The following night he hosted the Ramseurs at his apartment and made them a dinner of mostly take-out.

"I couldn't help wondering if that silky voice who called Friday was your gal," said Ramseur.

"Button called you?"

"Button, now a name like that put to a voice like that, why you *must* tell me about her," purred Carolotta. Her body English had her husband in a trance, and it worked on Randal too.

"She's a poet I met when we covered the Regional Writers Awards, and she lives in a mountain hamlet up near the Tennessee line. Her parents are hippies, like y'all used to be, except they still look it," said Randal. He dug a picture out of his wallet.

"She appears to be a Native American," said Tarleton. Randal laughed.

"She's as much an Indian as you are: member of the Rolling Rock tribe."

"Speaking of which," and Ramseur left the table. Carolotta seized Randal's hand and steadied her gaze.

"I'd love to meet her," she said. Ramseur returned with bottles and glasses.

"Problem is, she's up there and I'm here with this Police Blotter crap—"

"Whoa now, son" said Ramseur. "While I concur with that demotion, it has a wide jurisdiction. What you seem to overlook is that we have the biggest readership in the state. Why? Because we cover the state from east to west, and many smaller papers are under the umbrella, ours included. Now, miss Springfield is surely a fox, if my darling wife will pardon the euphemism, so you ought to be closer together. It was me, I wouldn't dawdle for a second. Why don't you sign up for evening classes a couple days a week? They won't require the stats that prevented your admission before; then you could ease on in as a full-time student."

Randal looked at his mentor but saw the seam of a sutured wound, a spirit annealed.

~ ~ ~

The next morning Randal drove to the city jail with 7-11 booty and was soon seated opposite the wily Welch. As before, he had to kick it off.

"Tell me more about the Beige Aryans and how they figure into things."

"Well, I can tell you this. Butch is a smart man. It wasn't him got caught was it?"

"Where is he now?" Randal knew it was the wrong question and held up his hands.

"You damn right I won't. Besides, that isn't his real name, and they never going to catch him anyway. He's way too smart; he can tell the time of day by looking at the sun, but me, I've never been able to make out the numbers."

"But you can talk about him without turning him in, right?" Welch thought it over while lighting up. He smoked. Randal waited. The guard stared. All was as it should be in jail.

"What he did was hide us from our enemies by changing our name. He'll change it again, too. The Brotherhood wasn't going to drop it. Phil was too important," said Welch.

"Who is Phil?"

"Philosophy, man, what we disagreed on; they wanted us dead. So, Butch got us hooked into this union that supports groups like us; you could be deconstructed and still have a life. So, we dropped the BA and started calling ourselves Better Us Than Them."

"That would be, uh B.U.T.T." said the intrepid reporter.

"You dis it and I'll kick *yours* into next week."

"What about the web site?"

"We left it up just to piss off our former brothers. The new name had no past, you know? Gave us a clean shot at a new start"

A new start at armed robbery thought Randal, a new beginning with getaway cars.

"That union helped us out. We were connected with lots of other groups too. You heard there's safety in numbers, right, well there's money too. Got to where we enforced the union rules, but it wasn't enough for Butch. He said we had a bigger plan; we needed more money to help out this group that was waiting for a space ship. B.U.T.T. is new age, man."

Randal sat up and flipped through his notes. Welch alone had been caught after a foiled heist in Statesborough and implicated in a host of others in eastern Tennessee and western North Carolina, holdups that had established a pattern, a modus operandi.

"This group you mentioned, did you ever go there, you know, to check them out?"

Welch sensed a change in the room, and it wasn't the approach of the guard so much as the reporter getting uppity; reminded him of a dog. He scooted back his chair and stood.

"You put my name in a story, or you don't get another word. Bring copies and this too." He handed across a list before being escorted back to his cell.

2

Jensen Tarbush was also contemplating a name change, one that would give him greater autonomy in the pursuit of justice. When he went after evildoers, he would be on his own and unsupported. He'd read about animal rights activists who'd been booted from their college for setting loose lab rats that ran amok in frat quads. If you carry the name of your sponsor, he reasoned, you cannot stray too far afield. His own wouldn't be a campus chapter; he would be his own and thereby write a new one in the annals of the movement. *Parasites Rights* was, even though not as yet formally chartered, on the books somewhere. It nagged and gnawed at him because it wasn't only parasites that were in danger, but the whole microcosm, and he, merely the son of a Baptist minister. It also dug at him because sloganeering wasn't his thing, but after weeks of word-play, he had come up with: PETPEv. It was too big a mouthful, he thought, but if you didn't trip over the words, it would get your attention. The logo would come later, but first there was a project to *button* down. Having cooled off, he couldn't feel the same sense of outrage, nor did he feel hurt anymore, although he tried to conjure up a wounded heart, but was stymied by the recurring thought: What a hot babe she is, and from my own town too. We'll see each other around, so just play it cool. Take the wise approach, the way dad would do it and convince her morally that selling edible bugs is making a deal with the devil. She'll come around, or maybe take it to her parents. They're supposed to be new age, even though dad despises them, but it's hard to think of anyone he does like besides mom and the Sheriff. I'll go after her customers. I'll shut them down: waylay their wheels and liberate the freight. Maybe they'll shop elsewhere, online, but at least Round Wilson will be rid of a pestilence on pests, and Button and Blue Jay Way will see their customer base dry up.

He pondered what little was known about the star gazers who had rented out the Rainbow Ruin, as it was known. There had been a lot of gossip and then it died down. The hippies, Button's parents and their friends, had built that place before he was born, and its dome had been a fascination as he grew up. Everybody went up there at one time or another, to party or make out or go all the way. It was a secret he had kept from his father, one of many. He got to work and outlined a plan slated to begin during the Christmas break when he was home.

~ ~ ~

Randal went in to see his boss and was waved to a chair. He sat and listened to the speaker phone where a string of callers got chewed out for daring to speak to the great and powerful Oz, Poke Madison. Randal sat on his hands and waited his turn. It finally came.

"Make it quick, Poe, I'm busy."

"Yes sir, the bank robber caught in Statesborough two weeks ago is—"

"Nobody, that's who. He's invisible and he's going to remain invisible."

"He's on to something bigger, I've—"

"He's a con and he's conning you: end of story. Thanks for stopping in." The senior editor of the Mountain News punched the speaker phone and growled as Randal withdrew, and once out in the hall, he texted Ramseur on his cell. He didn't know where else to turn. His phone rang.

"Listen, you've got to look at the practical side of it," said Ramseur, "ask any other veteran. Most felons will pump you full of hot air if you let them. They've always got a tale to tell, but if you really listen you will hear every urban myth rehashed and resold, but with a twist, and that's the catch, the inside line that only they have on the situation. But hey, it's fertile ground for journalism. I started there, and so did that man you just spoke to."

"I didn't speak to him at all. It was the other way around. He reminded me of my dad, a one-way stream of gruff. I'll bet he talks that way to his wife."

"You might be surprised. I happen to know her quite well."

"Oh hey, I didn't mean—listen, Mr. Ramseur, I've got a feeling I'm on to something, but I've hit a wall unless I can show this guy his name in print."

"Take him copy. He's feeding you: you feed him. As to the other thing, I wouldn't sweat it. You stay in this business long enough you'll be just like him."

~ ~ ~

The following day Randal checked his blotter assignments before heading to the jail, but he made a few stops that included Kinko's for a little desk top publishing razzle-dazzle, and to flirt with a clerk he knew. He described his main problem and toyed with another, but she was all business.

"Who's that tub I've seen you with lately?"

"He's an old friend," said Randal.

"Yeah? Circling the drain, I'd say."

"He mentored me much in the way I'm mentoring you."

"Hard to see how drooling and journalism fit. These margins look right?"

Randal sat at the interview window and spread his wares on the counter. Welch shuffled in and collapsed into the chair, yawning, but perked up when he spied the carton of Marlboro beside a stack of newspapers. He stared at the article and lit one smoke after another.

Randal waited in the cloud, wondering if bank robbers had time to read between heists, and what genres.

"This is righteous brother Poe," said Welch.

"Where's my other stuff?" Randal slid them beneath the partition as the guard's head loomed into view. Welch tore open a bag.

"I'd like to ask about that. The package says that Caterpillar Crunch is a combination of trail mix and roasted caterpillars. Seems an odd snack," said Randal.

"Hard to get stir-fried mealworms in here."

"I guess this stuff is easy to carry on the run," prompted Randal.

"My favorite is Spicy Jack Cheese with Grubs, but man, this is tits."

"So, ah, you ever carry beef jerky? The Bugg twins always had it," said Randal.

"Yeah, but look at their skin. Butch made a rule about that. Sent us a red flag email." Randal nodded, urging him onward without appearing too eager to gain an edge.

"Was after we hit that bank in, well never mind, but the guard couldn't get his gun out. His hands were slick with deep-fried wax moth larvae; had it all over him, in fact. That wasn't a chance thing, no sir. We don't just case the bank; we case the people too."

"Suppose the guards don't go for the bugs, they're not like French fries."

"They don't have a choice; you see we got this device that sprays it out."

"So, it's pretty greasy, huh?" said Randal.

"Depends on how you do it. Lightly fried it melts in your mouth, not on your Glock."

This set Welch to roaring and gave Randal a moment to jot notes. Butch seemed like an odd profile of a bank robber, the stereotype perhaps worn like a holdup mask, and Welch himself was a contradiction of health food and tar and nicotine. He had an idea.

"I can fill in a lot that's missing from that article if I had another source. Has anyone else been in here to pick your brain?"

"They keep interrupting my morning yoga with this FBI asshole. I give him shit, but he's already so full I can't see where he puts it," said Welch with a chuckle.

"I think I know who you mean. His name is the same as that lawnmower."

"It's Riggs, your thinking is wrong; what did you have for breakfast?"

"Well, ah French toast and coffee."

"I knew it right off. You get better protein in bugs, don't make you sluggish."

"You eat them for every meal?"

"That bread you ate could have been made with honeybee flour, but it wasn't. Don't get me wrong, sometimes I'd go ape shit and slop on a burger, but Butch changed all that, made me see the light," said Welch, who wistfully added, "a pearly light."

The guard loomed, and as instructed Randal waved a folded bill, slipped it under the plexiglass, and gained time to keep the interview alive.

"It sounds like if I had met this Butch, he would have changed my life too."

"Look at me, how old you think I am," said Welch. Randal named a number.

"Way off, I'm near forty. It's how you live. Who said New Age, well it goes back further than that, and so does Butch, but you wouldn't know it to look at him; his generation was the first to do all this shit."

"Well, I was referring to the spaceship connection with B.U.T.T.," said Randal, "that seems about as New Age as you can get."

"What I'm saying is that you wouldn't a met him; he's on remote."

"Remote . . . like what, radio or something?"

"No man, a cheesy web cam. He comes through the ether like it's another planet."

"I had the impression he was, well, with you," said Randal.

"You heard of distance learning? That's how he hooked us up with that group up there, they are way hip, but holier than thou, you know."

"No, not exactly, can you help me out?"

"Well, first off, they're very secretive. I mean a bank robber won't tell you jack, but these people are in a trance, took like two hours to get through their security."

"Butch didn't have pull?"

"He's just a blurry face on a monitor. Never did meet him. I think he's got a squeeze, an android mama, you know, and there's plenty of 'em there. It's funny to think on it now, those half-naked women, but they won't talk to you unless you're one of them," said Welch.

"I don't suppose you saw a spaceship." Welch regarded him, but Randal held up a hand.

"What I mean is if you saw anything unusual."

"Well, that place has some kind of sex energy. Most of the members like I said were half naked, some of them all the way. Their leader appeared on a cheap ass closed circuit TV that came and went. Said he was on Mercury. I think he was on something else, to tell you the truth. Everybody there, including the gang, watched his show in this huge room with a glass ceiling, like a big skylight. I didn't get any of it."

Randal stood at the approach of the guard.

"One other thing bro: that TV reception was pretty bad, but I'd swear the cult leader was Butch's twin. I think that's why we're funding them. Our contract stipulated one hundred tons of micro-livestock like what you brought me. That's a ship load of protein."

"Well, I thank you for your time," said Randal.

"That supposed to be a joke?" Welch went to his cell laughing, and Randal headed home.

~ ~ ~

On the living room wall of his apartment, he tacked a road map and decorated it with push pins. Each pin would represent one of the B.U.T.T. holdups and he hoped to know that it would broaden his perspective of whatever it was he was onto. He was certain he had a fix on something, just as he had many times before. His friend and mentor, Tarleton Ramseur, had once called him a bloodhound for stories, and had banked it to Randal's benefit, first getting him hired at his own Raleigh paper, the flagship of the one he now worked for. He sank the last of the pins and stood back. A ragged circle was formed from the locations of holdups in eastern Tennessee, western North Carolina, and south western Virginia. With a compass Randal figured distances and guessed without looking that Round Wilson stood at the center like an axel on a wheel, each spoke running out about two hours distant, give or take. He thought of reporters in nearby towns as well as those whose local knowledge might shed some light, those who seemed the most open and generous, and he also tagged Cody Springfield as a good bet, or his bud Jam, but he'd keep it away from Button if he could. For the time being, and with the Christmas holiday approaching, he wanted nothing more from Button than the lady herself. He was but one among many with amorous plans.

3

In Round Wilson Millicent Tarbush busied herself with a casserole and thoughts of LA and counted the hours to their next rendezvous, grateful that her husband was involved with the Tri-county Ministry and would be preaching that Sunday all the way down in Lumberville. It would give her fretless leisure and quality time with her darling. With her son in Ashville at college, and her daughter at school in France, she would be as free as a dove. A muttered curse from the den brought her back, but signaled, she would confide to LA, a déjà vu of that very moment grating cheese, as though she had stepped outside and watched herself through the kitchen window in an act less familiar than habitual.

The Reverend August Tarbush crumpled another sheet and started again. He wanted, no he needed to get it right. It had to be right, that must have been what she meant. People don't just engage in cryptic dialog without a reason; it has a purpose, an underlying message, not unlike a sermon, he realized. And that of course was the key. He would compose her message in the body of the sermon, and then skip over it in the pulpit. Her pulpit would of course be a different story, and he squeezed his legs together and tingled at the memory. She had been brusque and bitchy behind the counter and it had shocked him to mumbling like an oaf, and he had stumbled out. Maybe it was just that store with its incense always catching in his throat. Then, two days later in the parking lot of the Dairy Queen she suggested *he* apologize and that nursing grudges themselves needed nursing before brushing him off like yesterday's news, much the way she had in the aftermath of their first meeting. He listened for his wife's puttering, ever a strain on his concentration, and began again, but his thoughts ran in circles chasing each other in a widening gyre and every circuit roared past Rainbow Run. He gave up and with a keystroke opened a favorite, Sermon-maker dot com. Soon, he had a stew of the coined and purloined:

How can God be just and yet justify the ungodly? How can a just and holy God declare sinners to be righteous? This I ask you, brothers, to ask of yourselves, to seek the answer, to beseech it to be born unto you and yea though mightily you shall seek it and search for it, the answer cannot be found within. The answer cannot be discovered in quietude; nay the answer cannot be found inside of you. The answer cannot be a local one for it is to be issued from on high and that is where and only where ye shall seek to find that answer and any answer. And I have done this very thing. I have lifted up mine eyes and beheld the great joy of the world and listened and heard the word and wept like a lamb as the nurse prepared an enema as a fitting treatment for the bad boy—he backspaced bad boy and retyped: rude and disrespectful truant who has promised to be good and to please her if only she would depart from the heathen on the hill, if only she would abandon the faithless flower children, that flock of doubting Thomases and perfidious Peters and non-mellifluous Mary's, and Mary Jane too that we all know flowers up there in Bill Zebub's garden. For righteous they must be to have been here thus long and not been struck down, to have bred among us a passel of imps now run amok in our schools and not one of them smote with the fury of the vengeful God who we the truly righteous know how to worship correctly here in our finest on the finest day of the week. Well, I tell you brothers that in my deepest vespers I have heard the whisper of the lord and he sayeth unto me that it is high time that the wicked shall wither and perish like the marked down fruit at the farmer's market, that it is high time that the wicked shall not be longer among us, that the wicked shall be sent from us and back to whatever bog they crawled from, or what planet may have deposited them upon our hills and vales, aliens from another time and place that speak in tongues and—

"Augie, will you have the Lite Cottage Cheese? I can't recall the doctor's orders," said his wife from the door. He hadn't heard it open so fervent was his appeal, the testimonial running on its own output, creating its own gravity and so suspending time, but now the spell was broken, and he drooped in the chair, spent but with just enough left in him to delete the nurse line. Then there was the prospect of dinner with Millie and her chatter that some time ago, and it wearied him to recall how far back it went, had failed to guide his interest. They seemed to be alone together only at meals now. Only as his protégé did they interact, but then, that was altogether a different story. Otherwise, she had her ongoing arrangements with the floral society, her socials and teas, and often as not away down in the valley where her mother in failing health ruled a kingdom of trailer parks. After he had arrived in these mountains, she had seemed the perfect catch: she had money and a higher sense of the value to be found in spending it virtuously; she was a serious young woman untroubled by the troubles of the age, a claim he could neither make nor escape from up until the time, about a week before his arrival in Round Wilson, when he had mistakenly donned a matching coat in a bus station washroom and many miles down the road found in the pocket a Roman collar. It seemed at the time one of those chance occurrences too prophetic to pass on, a message sent that he was departing from one ministry only to enter another, although quite different in its embrace and its reach. Once he'd donned the collar, he became a different man, and he stopped looking back. When he married Millicent, he also wed a community and with it a cloak of respect. If he had a back trail, it didn't extend to the aisle between the pews. They settled in, raised a family and made a life on the slopes of Mt. Gertrude, as did a group of hippies recently arrived from New York.

The new Reverend treated them with disdain from the outset, wanting the distinction established early on that while he too was young and bearded there the parallel ended. The last thing he needed were random traces turning up connections. Thus, did he befriend the Sheriff and others and preach fire and brimstone against nonconformists, and Yankee ones at that, living in crude shacks and teepees and building a barn in which to gaze at the stars while he and Millicent established themselves as pillars of the community and set about making sure that everyone knew it. But now, he wasn't so sure about his wife or his marriage, and he fretted that his well-crafted image might slip of a sudden, as surely it had with that little fox from Blue Jay Way. But he would have her, oh yes, and whatever play she directed he would act in, for the drama she brought to the stage of his being was like none other. By the looks of it, it would be a Christmas play because that's when local kids away at college would next be home, his son and his love. If only I could use him to keep an eye on her down in Ashville, but he's a square peg if ever there was one. The reverend saved the sermon, stood and stretched, and followed his fate to the dining room.

~ ~ ~

A few miles west it was also dinner time at the compound of the Mystic Knights of Moonstone Light, and Delray Mabler had ordered in; he didn't care to leave his room for two reasons. The first and more notable was Mrs. Nungesser who could bend him like a spoon, but the better was that he was reading a book he couldn't put down, Argon's magnum of time travel and the search for wrinkle-free gravity that had so far transcended generations. He was interrupted by a knock on his door, and after verifying that it wasn't the love tap of the mammoth mademoiselle he sat back with a sandwich and went on reading. Argon's character, Zarkassadi was then hatching a plan with his sidekick, Seshundhance, to mend a worm-hole in the universal fabric with homemade plasma thread woven from consciousness as it passed through an electromagnetic grid suspended in a frame made from cast off *waffle irons* as they were then called, the antennae of second-hand space ships.

Mabler put down the book and finished his dinner, pondering his wife and son, as distant to him now, it seemed, as his host's characters in outer space. He picked up the phone, requested an outside line, and called his wife. But just as before and every time he'd called, his mother-in-law's voicemail came screeching into his ear like a wounded cat. Well, he was going to have to do something about this. Taking refuge was a reflex and he had jumped at the chance. But now, things may have cooled off, he reasoned, including his wife, and cooler heads would prevail. He would speak to Argon about borrowing a car. Meanwhile, he needed to get the news, for up here they were limited to Argon's own broadcasts and no one seemed to pay it any mind. But Mabler wanted to know what was going on, and particularly as it concerned him; was he yet a hunted man? Perhaps it was the thought of driving away, a sudden departure that caused him to reach for the book and open it to the end. What he read there in the final pages shocked him to his toes: Argon had written of his own arrival as a prophesy come to pass, but when Mabler traced the footnote to an earlier page he found: *Insert Elvis here*. He read on, forwards and back, skipping about, and discovered that the story had led to this mountaintop retreat but from that point onward it was like a journal: He's making it up as he goes along! The predictions Argon made were all accurate, but they were recorded in the pages of his book; he can't read the future until he has written it first! Mabler was saddened that the story would lose its grip on him so fast that he became disinterested in the further escapades of the author, Argon himself, who now seemed to be dealing from the bottom of the deck. But even so tainted, the intervening yarn still drew him and so he returned to the bookmark and ploughed ahead. The two heroes were soon on their way to a place called Black Hole in the Wall in order to recruit accomplices to rob an Aquarius plasma bank; they needed more of the precious stuff. As he read, an idea came to him on how he could get into town for a reconnaissance and he bookmarked his own prediction.

4

In another part of the town a man sat listening to a tape recording and transcribing passages on a yellow legal pad. Harlan Riggs had picked up the tape that afternoon on his way back from a weekend down east. His request for a wiretap had been delayed by a sleepy judge and sloppy installation in the interview room at the county jail and so had not captured the initial exchanges, but what he had learned from the tape convinced him Howard Welch held a valuable key that could open the rusted locks on an age-old case that had taken thousands of man hours of research and slogging detective work, much of it his, and gone nowhere except the cold case files. It was a blemish on a record otherwise unmarked, that is if one could overlook the lost trail of the garbage bomber Ralph Bannister. But now a jailed bank robber had told Randal Poe about a machine that spewed goo! He checked the lab report from the bank heists: the sprayed-out substance was shown to be an admixture of three components: fryer grease—no help there, the poor man's biodiesel could be obtained at any restaurant; 10 W 30 motor oil, again no help, but the third item stood out and by its very oddity made it suspect: granulated arthropoda of the genus Romalea. Where previously he'd scanned, he now read each detail: antennae, labrum, palp; thorax: all sections; abdomen: wings, femur, tarsus, pulvillus, ovipositor, pharynx, and followed by a superscript parenthesis in which a lab tech had hand written: *to wit>pulverized grasshopper*. Could that be the link? He needed more, and he shuffled paperwork and found the folder of old notes, memos, and briefings, and ran a jaundiced eye through it all, having read and reread it all many times, sifting for that overlooked iota on which cases often hang. He recalled with distaste those times it seemed he had found it, only to come up empty once again.

The casing of Bannister's lethal projectile had been not merely an acorn squash, but an organically grown one, and the agency had gone all out on that angle. Area health food stores had been thoroughly cased but the profiles suggested a different brand of hippie, those given to an overthrow of gardening, not government; but in their midst stalked an outsider. Many were questioned and a few tailed but it all came to nothing, and the agency abandoned the organic link, but Riggs had carried on, having become an avid gardener himself.

It was his subscription to gardening magazines that had led him out here to the sticks where he'd taken up station. A frequent contributor signing himself R. B. had submitted dozens of articles over the years to periodicals such as *Basal Basil* and *The Organic Mechanic.* Riggs had been unable to obtain subpoenas and been chewed out for following a long-abandoned lead and had settled for the only thing that ever really seemed to work. Brandishing faked court orders that he never allowed them to see, he browbeat editors into verbal admission that the so-called R.B. had mailed his articles from Ashville, North Carolina. Riggs closed the file and chided himself for the millionth time; R.B. could be anybody!

Coming back to Welch, Riggs also saw that another key was available locally, that there was a way to get around Welch whose code of silence was the sort of wall he could never breach. He contemplated the odd juxtaposition of gang members and the ethics that bound them to each other as well as to their own insularity; it was almost admirable. If only it was matched by civility and a healthy dose of the golden rule, but such are the hallmarks to be found in the likes of our journalist Mr. Poe, he reasoned, as he rewound the tape and checked the second item on his list, then headed for his truck.

He drove the switchbacks over to Asheville and parked up the street from the apartment and understood he wouldn't have long to wait for he already knew the kid's general pattern. Like many, Poe worked and then went home; the only deviation from what appeared to be a static lifestyle was his recent enrollment for evening college. Riggs opened the Starbucks Latte and took a hit and thought how Poe and Welch seemed to parallel each other, both incarcerated in a stagnant and predictable existence. The signal difference was that Poe had people 'on the outside' with whom he shared his life. Mainly, there was the Springfield girl, and a damned good connection that would prove to be. Thanks son, you're going to make my job easier. Poe arrived on foot and entered the apartment. Riggs finished his coffee and stepped from the car and soon after rang the bell.

Randal answered the door.

"Hello, my name is Harlan Riggs. May I come in?"

They sat in the living room.

"So, what can I do for you? I've seen you around," said Randal, "but places we don't often associate with real estate development. Is that a side line?"

"You're pretty sharp," said Riggs.

"Part of my job; I get paid to notice things."

"Hmmm, anything caught your eye at the jail?"

"How do you mean?" said Randal. It confirmed his sightings of Riggs there, once in the lobby and once upstairs where access was limited to those on police business.

"I think you know what I mean," said Riggs.

"You're going to have to tell me who you are," said Randal, and then eyeballing the badge thought, ah, Welch's interrogator that wasn't getting anywhere with the bank robber.

"I repeat the question," said Riggs.

"He's a good conversationalist."

"I don't have that impression," said Riggs.

"He is a live wire."

"He's just another dipshit with a sheet," said Riggs. "He had a string of warrants on him a mile long."

"Well, I can see that he is no saint," said Randal, "but he has redeeming qualities."

"He'd stab you in the back for a dollar. The only thing that's redeeming about people like Welch is the repayment of their debt to society. He won't see daylight until his ass grows a new set of legs."

"And the tax payer foots the bill," said Randal. He had no stake in arguing but there was something about Riggs that rubbed him the wrong way.

"Keeping them locked up is the point, son, and it is worth any price. Anyway, the screws tell me he's a real songbird when you're there."

"We get along pretty well. Turns out we have friends in common," said Randal.

"That would be the Bugg brothers, you don't want those kinds of friends," said Riggs.

"Small world." Randal got up and went to grab a beer. He didn't offer Riggs one.

"Here's the deal Poe: I want everything shit-bird told you."

Again, Randal thought, why not, his source didn't need to be protected, and as the agent pointed out, Welch wasn't going anywhere. But all the same, what was it about Riggs? Was it the cheesy windbreaker, they always seemed cheap, or the mustache? He couldn't put a finger on it, but all the same he felt like giving Riggs the middle one.

"Damn it, son, don't piss off the wrong people." Still, Randal hesitated.

"You go about your job day to day and live in this shithole apartment and think you're doing fine. But we still have a file on you from that hog farm thing where you piled up felonies like firewood," said Riggs, a little flushed.

"I think you'd better leave, Mr. Riggs. I'm not going to sit here and be harangued. Maybe people won't talk to you because you abuse them."

"You're not hearing me. You give me every damn syllable of Welch or I'll find something to charge you with. You got that?"

Randal had gotten up and opened the door and stood beside it until Riggs brushed past him on his way out. Only then did he notice his hands were shaking.

He called Button and was disappointed to get her voice mail, then checked her schedule and decided to hike over to the campus. The brisk air would do him good; clear his head of the noxious fumes left by Special Agent Riggs. Special at what, he thought, being an asshole? This thought cheered him, and he lengthened his stride and encountered memories special to the occasion: his reporting on and interviews with the Honeycutt clan at Hogville that befriended him to the family, and they had treated him like one of their own, so allowing him to write a clearer and more accurate account of their stake, their livelihood. It had been his first professional gig as a freelance journalist, although his mentor had chided him over breaking the cardinal rule of interviewing: never get too close to your source. How true a maxim it had proved to be when his phone call to the environmental hotline had cast the first stone of an avalanche that had destroyed the farm and ended their heritage in hog farming. Then, in an attempt to salvage his honor, as much as that of the devastated Honeycutts, he had led the farmers on a raid of the state facility that quarantined their swine and guided the rolling convoy toward the hills, these hills in fact. He looked off to the west where forty miles distant lay the village of Bluff and the final resting place, if you could call it that, of his father. Loudspeakers awoke him from his reverie, and he headed for distant banners flapping in the breeze.

~ ~ ~

The gathering announced itself as "The Green Consortium" and it was slated to host a number of campus organizations that appeared to be ranked in popularity, starting from over on the left where Greenpeace staffed a lively booth to the middle section where the crowd milled around several state groups decrying the vanishing Outer Banks and on over to the right end of the line where a lone figure struggled with a clutch of handouts to hold aloft a banner that read, PETPEv: *People for the Ethical Treatment of Pests, Everywhere*, but the banner kept catching wind and his awkward gesticulating reminded Randal of an orchestra conductor, but the lone audience member was wearing a parka he recognized, along with her inky hair spilling from a purple toboggan. He went over and stood beside her, but she was too engaged to notice him.

"Look, Dingle, it's just a small family business. You know yourself how vital cottage industry is in a mountain town."

"Nothing is quite so vital as death!" said the boy with his arms up.

"We also have Jam who fixes things for folks, their cars and stuff, and we sell a lot at the farmer's market," proclaimed Ms. Button Springfield, proud of her parents' lifestyle.

"Blue Jay Way is a death merchant! You and your family are peddling death!"

"I pedal my bike, get real," said Button.

"We know that you're selling death to that cult."

"You're as weird as your father," she said, and turning to go, she bumped into Randal.

"Oh hey, sweet!" she said, and planted one.

"Hey yourself; Is this guy bothering you?"

"You hungry? I know a place has great *beetle burgers*," she said over her shoulder at a glaring Jensen Tarbush, president, secretary, and treasurer of PETPEv.

"What was that all about?" said Randal.

"He's a geek from home," she said.

"Who is his old man?" he said. They walked some ways before she answered, a wry smile curling the corner of her mouth as she recalled previous encounters.

"He's alternately a worm and a revivalist," she said.

"It doesn't seem like you'd know a preacher."

"In Round Wilson, everyone knows everyone. When you came to visit, I was going to show you the sights, but you yawned and missed 'em."

"It's not small on charm, though."

"Remember our cave, you could put the entire population in there and have enough room left for the pied piper to dance," she said.

Randal sensed a hint of bitterness in the crack.

"But not Rainbow Run," he said. "And did you ever find out about the chanting in the cave?"

She squeezed his hand and smiled at him as they entered the Student Union.

"Gert was gonna to look into it," she said.

"The lady with the bear," he said, as though ordering an item from the steam tables before him.

"The lady *and* the bear," she said. "Randal, how about looking into that for me: I'll call her. I've got too much to get done before the break."

It seemed an odd request as the town was only twenty miles away, but there was something else he wanted to check on there, so he didn't give it another thought.

5

Jam down shifted the old Econoline van as he wheeled around another switchback, the curtains behind him swinging with the motion. He had bought the van new in 1964 with the proceeds from a very good year in the Cannabis trade and hadn't done more to it than change the oil. The paint had faded like the hair on his head, but he mused they were both still chugging along. He backed up the steep drive way and tapped the horn, and soon after was depositing his freight at the Mystic Knights loading dock. Okay, that's about it, fifteen kilos of Taragon Termites. The clerk checked the requisition slip and pointed out an error, and the two went inside the shipping office to confer.

As he drove back down the mountain he nearly flew from the van as a hand gripped his shoulder.

"Holy shit! That kinda mojo doesn't get it!" Jam pulled to the shoulder and stopped.

"I'm sorry, really, but see, I need to get away from there without calling attention."

"Making a break, huh? Wonder why I never see anyone leave."

"They come and go, but it's different for me."

"Why don't you sit up here." The man was reluctant, but Jam coaxed him forward, and he crawled over the engine cover, lowering the visor as he sat.

"Another surprise," said Jam, "I thought you died up there in Nashville."

"It's not that simple. Listen, would you happen to have a hat?"

"There's a mess of stuff in that glove box and behind the seat. You're as likely to find that as anything."

Delray Mabler let out a sigh of relief as he put on the pair of aviator sunglasses.

Jam took off his gimme cap and handed it across. "Melton Jeffries, but everybody calls me Jam." They shook hands, and Jam thought, any fugitive has a right to privacy. If he won't give it up, I won't abuse him of it.

"Look, I empathize with your ordeal, and I can drop you pretty much anywhere, just name it."

"What I need is news. That place is in a blind spot for radio waves," said Mabler.

"I doubt it. We live just the other side of that ridge, and we get good reception, but then, we don't need it, don't live by it."

Mabler gained another insight on his host and the secretive nature of his followers.

"Well, locally we've got the library. They'll have the regional papers; otherwise, I can run you over to Asheville."

"The library here should do fine. Thing is, I need to get back up there incognito. Could you wait? I will have no other way. I can pay you."

"You know, back then I wasn't in to you at all; it was a different scene. For me it was the Airplane, the Dead, Quicksilver, you know, and the cats that picked up where the Beats left off, but I respected you none the less, so it's kind of a thrill to be in your debt even though you probably see it the other way around. What I'll do is go drop off these crates and pallets and swing back by here in like an hour or so. You don't see the van I'll be out back. Anything I can get you, meanwhile?"

Mabler entered the library and glanced around, but there was only a young man chatting with the librarian and children's voices coming from the stacks. He removed the shades but left the hat on and took several newspapers from the rack before sitting at a table near the front windows and paging through them, but there was nothing about him in the Ashville or Lumberville papers. So far, so good, and he eyed the librarian, waiting for her to finish with the customer, but they went on and on like old friends. He decided to risk it and approached the desk. The woman turned to him.

"Excuse me, I was wondering where I might find a Charlotte, Greensboro or a Winston-Salem newspaper," he said, fiddling with the glasses so that his hand shielded his face. It didn't help, as the young man turned toward him with a smile, a smile of recognition, and it was pasted to the face of Randal Poe, the absolute last person he wanted to run across just then, or ever.

The librarian addressed him.

"Well, you just cool your heels a while and the papers will be here like always, right around ten. They are already here, of course, out by the parkway, but our delivery man is getting on in years. You will choose between either Charlotte or Roanoke Rapids. In the meanwhile, why not peruse the latest arrivals from the grand world of publishing?"

Mabler felt cornered, but something in Poe's eyes lowered his guard, and where could he go now, anyway? He sat back down at the table, his head in his hands.

"Now, as I was saying, Button is my god daughter and a very special person to me. We are very close, and that positions you rather nicely, at least for the time being. She speaks highly of you, even though the two of you have not known each other very long."

"I feel as though I've known her all my life."

"She has that effect on many, but her wisdom works both ways."

"I don't follow," said Randal.

"Button is a will o' the wisp, and what she sees in you she values, but she also sees beyond you and on into other realms of which mere mortals can but dream."

"You're suggesting that what we share is for the short term?"

"Perhaps, but if your love is strong enough, who can say but the wind?"

Randal had been speaking to her for twenty minutes and had gotten no closer to the purpose for his visit, primarily due to the librarian's verbal flights of discourse, and he imagined her unfurling parchment scrolls and sending aloft squadrons of iambs. He excused himself and went over to speak to Mabler before the man skedaddled, and pulled out a chair and sat down opposite the glum impersonator.

"Mr. Mabler, I want you to know that I am at fault. None of what transpired was any of Mr. Ramseur's doing. Further, I am deeply sorry to have caused you and your family any pain, and I am working to redeem myself in that regard." Mabler said nothing.

"I would like to help you in any way I can." He scribbled his address and phone. "Please understand that I am sincere. The loss of the interview was avoidable, but I was careless. Mr. Ramseur chewed me out for it, but I need to make it up to you. How can I help you?"

Mabler raised his head and glared.

"Alright, what media's been around here since you exposed me?"

"Well, the TV stations were on it pretty fast, but they left almost as quickly, as I understand it."

"What about right now?"

"There have been a couple freelance hacks camped out at the motel, but they may be gone. I can check it out pretty quick."

Randal got up and went to the desk, and as he was using the phone the doors opened, and an elderly gent came in with cardboard boxes on a hand truck. Mabler went into the gents and stayed there until the delivery man was gone, and then settled back down to go through the papers, and Poe returned to tell him that the freelancers were still there but they had been joined by a stringer from the Washington Post.

"There's nothing in any of these papers. Ask her how far back they keep these things," said Mabler.

Through the front window Randal saw a familiar van pull up at the curb, and it reminded him of his duties. He doubted that he would get much local information from the librarian, or if he did it would be swaddled in Byron, whereas the driver of the van out there was a more likely source and a hell of a lot easier to talk to. Even so, he gave it one more shot, and it paid off. Yes, the mountain had been known to *sing*, or at least sing was the closest translation that could be found in very dated Algonquian scripts compiled by some of the earliest anthropologists' field research, but there was also local lore. Myth had it that an Indian maiden whose heart was broken by the death of her lover who had slipped crossing a high waterfall and fallen to his death, threw herself into the same chasm rather than go on living without him. The two were put into a mound burial that grew with every passing moon until it was the mountain now called Gertrude, and that in certain seasons you could hear them crying, or singing, depending on who was telling the story. Well, that certainly would help Button, who had been intent on returning for further spelunking. For Randal, the only fun in it had been the bumping blind groping of each other as they felt their way toward a climax that warmed him to recollect. What other reason to keep the lantern turned off in that cramped and musky tomb? When he turned away from the desk, Mabler was gone, and so was the van. Hmm, now there's an interesting coincidence. Jam hadn't come in, nor had he left the van. He checked his watch. Better get back to Asheville and write up the day's copy. I can talk to Jam and Cody anytime, only a couple weeks until the Christmas break anyway, and then Button will be coming home and, in all likelihood, we'll be able to spend some quality time up here, sure do hope it snows.

"Young man, did you find out all you needed?" said Ruth Broadman.

"Yes, ma'am, I did."

"Well, I have the distinct impression that there is something else. Do ask. I have nothing much better to do this day," she said. Randal hesitated, but the reporter's instinct got the better of him and he rested his forearms on the counter once again.

"This is perhaps an odd departure from a singing mountain, but have there been any bank robberies up this way in the last several years?" He figured her local knowledge beat digging through newspapers like Mabler.

"Bank robberies, now that *is* an odd one," she said, "none here that I recall, although there was a robbery down in, what was it, Pinetop Ledge if my memory serves, and lately all it serves is dinner," and she gave him a theatrical wink. "The police found the getaway car down at the county line just sitting right in the road like it was a parking lot. It's a wonder a log truck didn't flatten it like a tin can, the way they are given to—"

"They find any evidence of the occupants?" said Randal.

"Wigs and women's hosiery, but an eyewitness said the driver was a big man. I know this because the chief of police over in Lumberville is an old knee knockin' buddy. Said it had to be a man because there was no woman that tall. Just goes to show you how a closed mind can mess you up. They had never seen women's basketball, I do believe."

"How about other holdups?"

"Give me a such as."

"Such as health food stores, sounds odd, I know."

"Well, well, that kind of thing won't raise eyelids around here, but it surely raised mine and here's why. These shops are like outlets. No, that's the wrong word, like mom-and-pop outfits; you blink and you've missed the inventory, but cottage industry is about the only industry up this way. A month or so back there were three of these places knocked over in the same week."

"Is that it?"

"Don't get uppity. I've got to line up my thoughts. Now, what they lost was what caught my attention in the first place: quartz crystals. One of these robberies made the paper. I got onto the others through the vine and that's how I know the other stuff taken was a bunch of New Age snack food. Probably it was kids, but *probably's* twin is *iffy*, and I've long been suspicious of that pair."

"On another topic, how much do you know about that group that rented the Celestial Center from Rainbow Run?"

"It gets curiouser and curiouser, does it not? So, you think these events are all linked."

Randal tried to backpedal, but it was too late.

"You may be a newspaper hound, sonny boy, but I can smell smoke when there's none in the air. Now, let's look at what we have."

A mother and her children came to the counter and Mrs. Broadman stamped the books and handed out candy with pleasantries and smiles, and then without skipping a beat returned her attention to Randal.

"Bank robbers and quartz thieves and a mysterious group, some say cult, encamped on yonder hill, and an Asheville reporter in lust with my goddaughter and a singing mountain to boot, and it all adds up to what folks around here like to call fodder; they'll spread it around and see if something grows out of it, but they lose interest pretty quick if it doesn't yield. I'm different. I believe that there is a thread running through just about everything that connects just about everything else. This one has got a hum to it. Can you hear it?"

Randal admired the metaphor but said that he had to go. She snagged his sleeve as he turned.

"I will do some poking around for you, young Mr. Poe, and the next time I see you we will rub elbows, and by the way, you can deliver this to Cody. It's already been here two weeks." She handed him the following year's edition of *Ye Olde Grange Almanac*. "You be especially nice to Button, you hear?"

Randal promised, and as he left the library for the drive back home, thought of swinging by Rainbow Run, but remembered Button telling him that Jam was often hard to locate; he had two cabins, one distant from the other, and sometimes lived in a converted bus, but that in the summer months he maintained a teepee down on Brindle Creek. Instead, he made another stop.

~ ~ ~

It didn't take too long to figure why Cody had denigrated the motel; it was a dump. Where better to look for hack writers, he thought, comparing the place to the one he had restored in Bessboro. He knocked at number 11. It was opened by a wide faced man with a white blanket wrapped around him like pastry dough, and whose breath rose in clouds. The room was colder than the air outside, and damp with mildew.

"Help you, sport?" said the man.

"I doubt it," said Randal, "but I can help you with this: you've been scooped." The man's eyes went wide as he grinned, but then narrowed to slits.

"Who says we've been scooped? And who the hell are you?"

"I'm Randal Poe with the Asheville Mountain News," and flashed his credential like that showoff Riggs. "I'm the guy whose filched interview started this side-show, you know that, don't you?"

The man nodded and took a step back and Randal followed him in but kept the door open.

"Well, I interviewed him again an hour ago, just before he headed out of town. You can read about it in the Mountain News. Have a nice day," and he went back out to his car but felt a tug on his coat.

"Listen, no harm done pal, I'm on a string like you. He say where he was going you could, you know, a professional favor. You know I can't cut out of here empty handed."

"I'll give you this much, he mentioned the Oregon Inlet," said Randal.

"Where is that, Oregon?"

Randal couldn't pass it up. "You might catch him, he's driving one of those canary yellow Hummers, part of the disguise. You hurry, you might catch him at the Tennessee line." Driving back to Asheville with the sun almost down, he felt at peace with himself and the world and felt that he had taken the first step on the road to redemption and figured he could locate Mabler pretty easily now, but it was odd Button hadn't said anything when they discussed his disappearance. Could it be that she didn't know he was camped at Rainbow Run? After all, she was in Asheville. Perhaps Cody forgot to mention it, but the time frame seemed askew. He was turning over these thoughts as he came up behind a log truck downshifting for the grade, and as they approached the stone archway emblematic of every interchange of the Blue Ridge Parkway, he saw Button's Beetle cross the span heading west, but he was already past the ramp before it registered. Where is she headed at this hour, he pondered, and swerved for a peek around the truck, but he couldn't get around it for miles, too late to try and follow her.

6

Button was chilled in the bug, its tiny heater cranked but emitting a whisper of heat. It didn't help any that the hospital whites were pretty thin but thinner still with nothing underneath, but it had to be that way; there wasn't going to be time to change. The overcoat did its best but her ankles, she imagined, were icicles forming from the knees. Yes, knees, and the shift in thought helped to warm her as she pictured her patient about to receive the sacrament. She drove into the lot and parked beside the Cadillac, and with her pass key (no, a church key opens a beer, says Jam) entered the vestibule in search of a knave in a nave, and she saw him then, suspended as per instructions and she strode forward removing the bag and hose from the overcoat as it dropped from her shoulders. She stood before him arms akimbo and said what a bad boy you have been, mouthing off to me at work and those lewd glares at the Dairy Queen. Well, well, we've got another kind of dairy for another kind of queen, don't we? He squirmed in reply as she bent to her task.

When commanded to let go he raced for the bathrooms behind the vestry. When he emerged a bit after, changed and combed, she sat waiting in a pew and putting on her best heartless gaze. She held out a hand to receive the tribute as per the usual end to their monthly soiree, but this time he broke the rules.

"I want you again, at Christmas," he squeaked.

"What! How dare you speak to me!"

"Oh please, Nursey Baton, I must, I need a special Christmas present," he whined.

"It's out of the question!" she said, buttoning the overcoat.

"Triple payment is what I will give, if you please."

"Is that right, well then, I'll take half of it now!" And again, she held out her hand. "And which will it be, Officer O, Nursey B, or La Domina, hmm?"

"I want an Indian Maiden, I want Pocahontas."

She laughed. "I think I can arrange it: dominant squaw and paleface captive, why not?"

They worked out the arrangements for the encounter and then she drove away with the tri-county collection warming her pocket in the frigid little car. Arriving back in Asheville she drove past her cottage once before doubling back; it wouldn't do to have to explain the nurse getup. In fact, much as she liked Randal, liked having him and having him around, she wasn't prepared to share the address book in her I-pod, and she reflected on how Cody and Amanda and Jam and all their friends too were promiscuous, fucking like bunnies, tasting each other, no proclivity denied, and they got along just fine with the world and everything in it, but they didn't tell all either, just made it seem so by their generosity. She knew some things about her parents that they were not aware of, some things they used to do, and especially her dad; she had gotten the message long ago that it was okay to have a secret world so long as it remained on the elliptical and didn't spin off its axis, and hers, she reflected, was sultrier than sin and safer than sex, yet considerably more lucrative than either.

She showered and toweled off, thinking: 'like everyone says, I've got the Native American part down au natural, like he's gonna get that far, but it's too cold for skimpy Indian duds, but where can I find a fringed leatherette burnoose?' She had the answer before she finished drying her hair: Ruth. She had all that stuff from the theatre that flopped and thought then how everyone in Round Wilson had played a part at one time or another, even Cody. He was the worst Indian ever and Jam, she chuckled at the memory, his Daniel Boone was so laid back that when he fought the bear it looked like he and Gertrude were dancing! They were, of course, but it wasn't supposed to look that way! And no less ghastly had been Mrs. Tarbush's French trapper's wife. Ever since her daughter had gone off to study in France, she had become a Francophobe, but her southern *bon jour* and *ca va bien* was so awfully drawled it was like she was speaking in tongues! No wonder the play never caught on. She made a cup of tea and a salad, and then turned on the desk lamp and opened her biology textbook.

~ ~ ~

The van idled at the foot of the steep driveway. Delray Mabler thanked the driver and handed back the sunglasses and the cap.

"I can't thank you enough."

"You're more than welcome. And hey, you know, you don't have to go back up there."

"Well, I do actually. It's a safe place for now."

"I've got a cabin so far back in the woods a GPS couldn't find it. You're welcome to it. I'm always willing to go the extra mile for a fugitive, doesn't matter what you're running from, what matters is *they* don't run faster, you know what I mean?" Mabler held his stare and nodded before he turned and started up the drive.

Argon met him in the entrance hallway and they exchanged pleasantries.

"I have been looking for you, sir," said the host.

"Well, even the king has to stretch his legs, you know," said Mabler.

"Sir, I must caution you that outside our gates we are not assured of safety. There are many in the valley that treat us with disdain, which is why we developed hiking paths up here. What trail were you on, the Laurel is my favorite," said Argon.

They strolled. Mabler reflected on the automatic gate, the guard, the chain link fence, the razor wire, the closed-circuit televisions and the general paranoia that bubbled beneath the surface like a caldera and wondered that his host maybe had it backwards.

"I wanted to ask you about your reading. Come across anything interesting?" said Argon.

"Your approach to the Mayan calendar mystery is a new one to me," said Mabler.

"You are familiar with them," said Argon.

"As the King of Rock and Roll, I have been asked a great many things, so my reading has been prodigious, but I took it for granted that the calendar stopped for more pedestrian causes, like they ran out of peyote or a new generation of seers said to heck with that jazz."

"Interesting, it's nice to compare the fantastic with the real; I never tire of it," said Argon, "but the facts, sir, will speak soon enough: the Elohim were writing the calendars and their departure and eventual return was and is no mystery. Let us consider what we know of birthstones and their Zodiacal force in the color chart of diluvian philosophy: What does January provide for us?" Mabler was relieved when Argon rolled onward:

"Amber, Turquoise, Zircon; February: Amethyst; March: Jade and Jasper; April: Lapis Lazuli and Sapphire; May: Agate, Chalcedony; June: Emerald and Green Feldspar; July: Malachite, Onyx, and Sardonyx; August: Carnelian, Garnet, and Ruby; September Light Green Serpentine and ah, I forget the other one, but it doesn't matter. October: we have Beryl, Crystal, and Diamond; November: Citrine and Topaz; December: I also forget."

Mabler recalled some of the names from the trays at Blue Jay Way while his host rambled on.

"Originally, it was the Elohim that crystallized these component parts and infused them with the force and the rhythm of Time borne across the Ayurvedic vector stream. The Mayans were but the scribes, the pencil pushers, but you see they simply weren't writing fast enough to keep up. Fortunately, medieval scholars recorded their own investigations via St. Jerome in the 5th century AD, based on the writings of one Flavius Josephus that held that gemstones wielded powers associated with their corresponding astrological signs and would proffer talismanic benefits."

Mabler was thinking about lyrics and how they seemed naked without attendant music; Argon's story line was designed for music only he could hear. "I am also curious about the mention of the Earth Mother."

"Ahh, you are perhaps even more perceptive than I," said Argon. "For that you must read on, and in Volume III her presence will be explained, unless she arrives before then. At any rate, the two of you, no—I will not give it away. Read on, Mr. Presley, read on," and Argon smiled and excused himself.

Mabler returned to his room to contemplate recent events as well as to undertake the next round of phoning Atlanta, convinced that enough voice mail would wear her down. In this round, each call would feature a verse of Love Me Tender subsequent to his entreaty; she would have to listen to the whole of it to get the gist and put together the puzzle pieces of his undying love. When finished he signed a few autographs from naked fans outside his door even though they looked far too young to have known who he hadn't been. He then called a local number.

"Is this Jam Jeffries?"

"You got him."

"This is the fella you gave a ride to yesterday. I was wondering if I might ask another favor."

"Well sir, if I can, I'll do it," said Jam.

Mabler explained his situation.

"I need to know if the coast is clear."

"I can snoop around a bit and see what's what, get back to you this number?" Mabler confirmed it. If the media had decamped, and Poe had seemed sincere, then there was no longer a need for him to remain in this glorified prison, and thought of the distant cabin offered by Jam and wondered if that too was a bit extreme. What he needed was his family back in his arms and all of them happy once again.

7

Harlan Riggs was thinking about family, too, but rather as a connected group of events that intersected somewhere nearby. He'd been around the area long enough now to have spoken to just about everyone, from café tables to rocking chairs to street corners he'd put together a picture that didn't fit what had from the start seemed the likeliest: the hippies were outstanding citizens who had proven themselves time and again.

They were standup. And thus far, the only connection he could find to garbage of any kind likely to make its way into a bomb was that of compost. They had a lot of it, but so did every farm. He had only one little thing to suggest that Cody Springfield was the real Ralph Bannister; Melton Jeffries was too tall by more than a foot, and none of the others came any closer to drawing even a filament of suspicion. But Cody had been teaching a class in organic gardening for the last nine years or so, and by God that had been enough to pique his interest, and one thing had come of it: many of his students, and some of them repeaters, had been drawn from the cult that rented their compound from Rainbow Run, but there the connection seemed to end, that is until a local journalist stuck his nose in. Poe was boffing the Springfield chick who, when not in school, worked in the family store that was supplying micro-livestock to the cult. But he had also learned (from the Sheriff) that the cult was buying the same product from an outside source and had in addition procured enough security equipment to fortify a military outpost; odder still, they didn't have a local bank account; when in town, they always paid in cash and departed quickly. The more he thought about it, the more hackles it raised until this latest wrinkle brought him back to bugs.

It had taken far too long to get the wiretap and he had missed a great deal of what had passed between Poe and Welch, but the tidbit he had now tipped the scales of suspicion: a shadow outlaw band, formerly with the AB and perhaps allied with them, was the outside source supplying the cult with bugs in bulk, and that info had been supplied by a bank robber. Well, that was enough, but he'd been rebuffed at the Bureau (as he knew he would be), reminded of his looming retirement, and was unwilling to forgo his cover just yet, for it had a basis in fact as there were land deals in the making, and next to that, regional key players knew him as a developer. He had made some solid connections, and there was money to be made. People don't like being duped; he could lose it all. Still, he could play it both ways by leaning on Poe, give him a Christmas present he wouldn't forget.

~ ~ ~

Also thinking about Christmas were thousands of students who were headed home for the holidays, some traveling to distant hearths while others would be home in an hour or so, such as Jensen Tarbush and Button Springfield who, among the last on campus, now stood in her snowy drive way.

"You can't just show up and ask for a ride!"

"I texted you," said Jensen.

"No, you didn't, no text, no email, no call, nada."

"Well, you can't just leave me here," he said.

"Look at the car, where are you going to sit?"

"You can leave some of this stuff here. Looks like you're moving."

"Jens, listen, you're really putting me in a jamb."

"I'll help you tie some stuff to the roof, make enough room for me to squeeze in," he said.

She didn't like it but she couldn't strand him there. And another sense tickled her as it had before, that here was the son, the offspring of the strangest creature, one she had once dared to ridicule and who had begged for a scripted humiliation that transgressed across a stage of what textbooks called sexual perversion, but that she oft referred to as bad acting, even as she had come to appreciate certain roles for their range of creativity. So, using rope with the other Tarbush, they made a space for him in the Beetle. They sat in the idling car.

"Now," said Button, "there will be no discussion of your pet peeve on the drive home, is that clear?"

"It's a big field, there's a lot to talk about."

"One word, one itsy bitsy word, and you walk."

"Well, I don't see as how we can avoid it. Besides, it's only an hour," he said.

"An hour drive is what, about five on foot. You'll be a frozen preacher's boy."

"So, what's he like?"

"Make sense," she said.

"That guy, the Mountain News creep."

"Why is it everything that comes out of your mouth reeks?"

"Alright, I'm sorry, it's just—"

"It's really none of your business. But even so, I will see him this evening."

"Well, I got over us, at least the love part."

"Jensen, there was no *us*, there was no love. Think of it as a passing cloud."

"We had something, I'm pretty sure of that."

She laughed. "Yeah, we had about four minutes of tongue. Don't turn it into a melodrama."

"But we had to break up. My old man would never have stood for it."

"And my dad wouldn't have stood for your dad! They're about as different as night and day, Cody as the light of reason; your father the whole of the dark ages."

"Yeah, well he has his faults, that's for sure, but it shouldn't stop us being friends."

It would if you knew what I know, she thought. "True, but what does stop is this other crap. I thought you had more sense."

"You said you wouldn't talk about it."

"Wrong, I said if *you* do—want to walk? Here's what you do, count Christmas lights until you see a yard Santa, then you have to bag them and start over."

As he counted, his thoughts ran to how he would be her friend and foe simultaneously and that she would see the light.

Button drove and thought how when boys got out of line, you had to be direct, and her thoughts turned to

Randal and she decided on a quick visit before they met up later and made a U-turn and headed for his street and cut the wheels to the curb when she saw the lights on in his apartment.

"Wait here," she said, and bounded up the steps.

"Hey, holiday girl!" They kissed, and she stepped inside and was introduced to the Ramseurs.

"Why yes," she said to Tarleton, "I remember you from the awards. It was one boss night."

"A night to be remembered, a great time had by all, I think, except for my charming wife who was unable to attend," and he and Carolotta bumped together.

"Well, I've met some great people since then; it opened a lot of doors," said Button who sat down beside Carolotta and the two soon had their heads together like old pals. Randal nodded to the kitchen and Tarleton followed, eager for a tour of the liquid supply.

"I may be off the blotter after the holidays."

"Poke won't keep you there too long, but long enough to see what you're made of, see if you'll quit, as some have," said Ramseur, leaning against the fridge.

"I think I'm close to breaking a story, a big one."

"You want to fill me in?"

"You backed up Madison by saying it's nothing at all, that it's a con," said Randal.

"Yes, well you get taken in by them, some are quite crafty indeed."

"This guy isn't sly so much as just, well, he doesn't fit the mold. I know, don't say it, but let's remember after Hogville I was in jail, not too long thanks to you, but a couple weeks was long enough to get the drift and with this blotter routine for months now, this guy is the only genuine article I've met; even the cops are phlegmatic. If you don't check the dullard box on the application, they won't hire you."

"Alright Randal, I'm all ears. Get us a beer first."

"You're the one guarding the cache."

"Okay, so give me what you have so far."

They clicked bottles, and Randal explained the series of interviews and talks with regional colleagues, and the stargazers and their connection to Rainbow Run and to Blue Jay Way and using his flagged state map on the wall over the kitchen table, pieced together the bank robberies with stats from police and press and lastly his discovery that a local real estate developer was in fact an undercover federal agent. When he came to the end, he noticed his audience had grown. Mrs. Ramseur and Button stood side by side, the latter glaring at him.

"Randal, I can't believe it! I left this bullshit behind only to come here and find you wallowing in it! Blue Jay Way sells good things to good people. What gives you the right to put it down? You think Cody's mixed up with bank robbers! This day began badly, and I am going home!"

"Baby, it's not Cody at all, he—"

Button shushed him by squeezing his mouth.

"Call me when you're ready to apologize. Don't ruin a good thing."

He was thankful that she didn't slam the door; her look was enough.

Carolotta hugged him, as Tarleton said, "This may be the wrong moment to say it son, but if I was you, I'd get an interview with this head fellow at, what is it, Python Knights? Use my name. We'll keep Poke out of it for now, see what you come up with, but sooner or later you'll have to tell him, and believe me, sooner's best." With that they left him nursing a beer while trying to figure it out; he hadn't said anything offensive and she was all over him.

~ ~ ~

The following day he called in sick and headed for the knob up behind Rainbow Run and its ultra-secret compound that up until then had minded its own business pretty well. But it seemed to Randal that whatever the business was, it was beginning to slop over the edges and involve a community that he sensed was wholly unprepared for its new role, and he imagined a younger Cody and Amanda and their friends lying beneath the dome and gazing toward the heavens; imagined the infant Button running between them and marveled at the beauty in it. But they had all grown up and the dome sat unused like a sleeping eye until it had opened again in another age. He slowed down for a hairpin turn and noted a Sheriff's department Jeep behind him, but when he pulled into the compound parking lot the Jeep turned around and drove away.

Following on what seemed like Fort Knox scrutiny at the gatehouse, he was ushered into a vestibule where he sat and thumbed a two-year-old Popular Science that he'd selected over a two-month-old Time on the assumption that out-of-date science would be more interesting than ancient news. Within an hour of proving his guess he became aware of a presence in the room, although he was alone. In a crack in the paneling, he perceived a movement, and springing to his feet a ruby fingernail scratched the fissure and vanished as the panel shut. 'Enough,' he thought, and walked out. On his way back down the ridge, he knew he wasn't headed home when by rote he turned into the corkscrew drive that led up to Rainbow Run and stopped at each of the three bridges, a ritual begun in a Button embrace. Whitewater danced and ran in a choral chant you never quite heard yet heard entirely when not listening but trying not to listen always put the mind in gear, and there was ever the wind. He chuckled and drove on and up into the turnaround in front of the main house where he was surrounded by yelping dogs.

8

Rainbow Run was the kind of place that grew on you. Maybe it was the bridges built of mortised walnut slabs, or was it the amber sandstone that lined the drive, or the water bars cut with a symmetry to the fall of the land, fluted in oak slats, or perhaps the plateau that opened at the turnaround, lined with Oleander, that gave onto panorama: a meadow as big as a Costco parking lot measured in weathered barns and stately trees. You got all that in Ashville's environs, he reasoned, but never all of it in one place, and then there were those who had made the place what it was. Randal parked his truck and was greeted by Jam.

"Hey Foot, what's loose?" They hugged.

"You're up just in time to help me out."

"Sure, is Button here?"

"Plenty of time my man, come on with me," and Randal walked across the meadow at an angle to the main house and passed two huts, smoke curling into cedars, and into a barn.

"You bootlegging?" said Randal.

"You buying? Here, let me show you," he said, setting up a step ladder that Randal dodged as he leapt to catch a beam where he hung long enough to marvel at the sight of hundreds of bottles in wooden frames alive with light, motes dancing in shafts. Dropping down he landed almost on top of Amanda. Another step and Kaboomb, baby. They laughed it up and hugged.

"You've seen the summer cache," said Amanda.

"What I've seen is—okay, what is that, honey?"

"Flirt with me a little more," said Amanda, as Jam came up.

"Son, this woman here needs a strong arm in a weak way."

"Well, I aim to please," said Randal, when Amanda swung him out of the path of Button on a charging pony that shot through the door and out the other side and then cantered back.

"Momma, you are the Sultress of this barn or of all barns? I *do* need to know."

Amanda vaulted onto the pony and they galloped away, observed by Randal who'd false-fainted into piled straw.

"They're a pair with no compare," said Jam.

"Hey, well one's enough for me," said Randal, who then followed Jam upstairs to the loft.

"Okay, but I gotta tell ya, Cody's pretty stuck on his gal." Jam handed bottles to Randal who loaded them into cardboard cases and stacked them.

"Wouldn't have taken y'all for moonshiners."

"It's Dandelion Wine."

"All of this is wine?"

"No, it's Dandelion Wine, from dandelions."

"Nah! I thought it was your dandy friends from Lyon. But how'd you pick so many?"

"Cody, Amanda, Bear and Cherry, Button, Me and La Linda and La Linda Two, and Jake, Jake's dad and Ulrike and her tribe and some elves from down by the bridges and a few more from where you hang, city cat," said Jam, as he descended the stairs and strode from the barn into sunlight.

Randal caught up with him. "You've been here from the start, right?"

"Summer of sixty-seven or eight."

"So, you've pretty much seen it all then."

"Seen a lot of what there's been to see, and so has she," said Jam, nodding at the purple nose of an old bus poking its silver grill out from under a tarp under a shed, International Harvester written across the hood in rust-pocked chrome. Jam led the way around it and opened the side door and they climbed into the mildew womb of a museum piece. Passenger seats once bolted in place had been removed and the interior remodeled and the metal framed windows looked hand painted in streaked pastels. Randal compared the interior to his dad's Winnebago. This one was home-made, and that other came from a factory readymade. This one held two couches, a counter with a sink and wooden cupboards and a dining table and four chairs beneath an oval ceiling of tongue and groove slats of a blond wood, and it fixated him as he recalled the plastic interior of his father's road yacht and its cigar reek that would never evanesce.

"We had a loft up there for a while," said Jam.

"For your luggage, huh."

"For us, bags and stuff went out here," and they stepped out of the bus and Jam poked a broom handle up under the tarp to reveal a narrow cat walk welded around the base of an elongated skylight louvered at both ends.

"S'funny thinking on it now, Round Wilson had never seen the likes of it, couldn't imagine what we were about. They musta thought we were from outer space."

"But now the people you rent to *are* from there, right?" asked the journalist.

"Well, I figure they're not too different than we were, just the times have changed, values, stuff like that."

"They could be very different, though. Do you ever see them, speak with them?"

"Well, there's one we deal with, comes to pay the rent every month. They don't write checks," said Jam.

"Is that the leader?"

"Nobody sees him, like Oz you know: Pay no attention to the man behind the curtain."

They settled on milk crates and leaned against the grill of the bus, a time traveler at rest. Randal could hear Button's shouts somewhere beyond the trees, and the galloping horses.

"Do you notice any odd behavior from them?"

"Define odd," said Jam, and patted the fender.

"Well, I mean like, do you hear chanting, or anything that comes to mind," said Randal.

"I've got a cabin just down the ridge from them. We used it as the kitchen and storage for the original dome, a bad idea come winter, but what did we know. Sometimes I hang out down there. Maybe I shouldn't say it, but I've seen a group of them, the same ones each time, changing clothes in a clearing by the road."

"Like work clothes or what?" Jam was quiet.

"This kind of runs counter to my beliefs, talking about people. We leave them alone, they do likewise; it's the nature of who we are. We're established here now, but it took a while. Virtue triumphed over prejudice, but it didn't happen overnight. Here comes your gal," said Jam and wandered off as Button sauntered across the clearing and as the two shared a hug, she looked over Jam's shoulder at Randal, and then walked over and sat beside him.

"Button listen, I'm—"

"Hey, you came out and talked it up with Jam and mom. No guilt trips, Randal. I appreciate it. I was going to tell Cody what you said. I wanted to start a fire; those people give me the creeps. They're far too secretive, and as such they add no value to the community," she said.

"Yeah, it defies the definition of community," he said, "on the other hand, these mountains tend to hold recluses, don't they? The mountains embrace them and no one's the wiser. Jam told me about his cabins way out in the wild, not that he's a recluse."

"Sometimes he needs to be and just disappears, but one of the cabins isn't all that far away," she said.

"Is that the one that used to cater the dome?"

"That place?" She looked him full in the face before she planted one on his cheek.

"I ran and hid in there once and they went frantic, called in every neighbor and the hills were crawling with people. I was fascinated that so many knew my name! Come on, I'll show you the one I mean," and she grabbed his hand. "See the broken fence over there? I'll race you to it," and she took off.

Randal bolted after her and caught up to her and matched her step for step until she winked at him and then he passed her by. They caught their breath at the fence before stepping through and then down the other side where the woods began and then climbed through rime dusted weeds as they skirted bramble thickets on the slope. When they reached a V shaped ledge, Randal found to his delight that toward its wider, fan shaped end were rows of Christmas trees, each looking quite prim in the thin, cold air.

"Do you get one every year?" he panted, a little out of breath.

"We don't do it that way. Show you later."

They began angling left as they rose higher, crossed a deer trail and then followed another as it went up through stands of walnut and beech and then across a meadow. Randal went at a crouch, fearful of scree, one of those slopes without an edge that seemed to lean over treetops. The trail leveled out as it entered a thick stand of laurel and as they emerged from it, he caught sight of a cedar shingled roof and then a window. Soon, they were leaning on the weathered railing.

"This is fantastic," he said, gulping air.

"Check it out from this side," she said. That view gave to them a long narrow defile of Brindle Creek as it dashed between boulders and fallen spurs, its banks thick with laurel. One side rose through a heavy stand of pine to a notch that bisected the adjacent slope, also covered in pine. Button pointed at the notch and then sighted down Randal's arm: just visible between the naked beech trees was a tall silver bullet topped with a glass nipple.

"What in the world is that," he said, though he thought he already knew.

"A secret they ought to share. Kids would love it; there's nothing like that up here anywhere. Park land would be preserved. We guessed they had sculpture in mind when Jam hunted up that nosecone. Cody's given them old tin he didn't need, other scrap."

"If it's so secret, why build it where they can be seen?"

"From here," she said, "we can only see the top twenty feet or so. From down there this cabin isn't visible, the angle, you know. But the weird thing, this cabin is downhill from the dome. It's the trees and ridges that keep it all segregated."

"That is weird, because the dome and Rainbow Run are at the same height, aren't they, but on parallel ridges?"

"Perspective is difficult in mountains," she said. "I'd guess that's why so many painters are attracted to the area; it is a true challenge to their talent."

They went inside the cabin and fired up the wood stove to make tea and warm themselves. When the stove was ticking and the room filling with heat they sat on the couch and tongue wrestled their merry way into peeling off layers as the chill dissipated. He straddled her, and she stroked him before placing him inside her like a guided missile, and piston and cylinder rocked together, and they chuffed and howled a primal countdown to ignition and a blastoff that jetted from Randal like a fire hose, and he collapsed against her spasms, as each one tightened them closer and deeper together while the stove clicked and the kettle whistled away.

Before they headed back, Button instructed him that they must leave something, a talisman for the next wayfarer, who may or may not be Jam, but that karmic tradition must be upheld. They searched pockets.

"I can't give up my lucky quartz crystal," she said.

"All I've got is a Susan B. Anthony half dollar, how about it?" Button put it in her pocket as the payment for directing him on how to lay a new fire in the woodstove.

Book Three

Anonymous Eponymous Parallax

Delray Mabler a.k.a. Elvis Presley, and by now a household face, made his way to the loading dock and in a reprise of his previous adventure stepped into the van and shut the rear doors behind him and before long it was winding down the mountain, Jam whistling a tune. By a prearranged pattern, he would deposit the cargo at the library and pick him up again an hour later, but this day would be a little different. They drove on past the library and kept going.

"Have you seen Ashville?" said Jam.

"Only time was a stopover. I seem to recall a café on a cliff," said Mabler.

"It has changed a great deal in recent years; no longer the sleepy college town."

"Well, I won't get to see much today. Just a quick meeting and a ride back," said Mabler, and he handed over the address Poe had scribbled on a sheet of paper.

Jam found it easily, and Mabler got out of the van and nodded to the driver.

"I can't thank you enough."

"Abyssinia," said Jam, wondering if the expression aged him at least as much as the forty-year-old van as he pulled it away from the curb.

Mabler rang the bell and was greeted by a startled Randal Poe. As they went inside, Harlan Riggs noted the arrival time of the van driven by the hippie he'd met at the farmer's market, and of the passenger whose face seemed familiar. He sat in his car and waited. An hour later the two men emerged and drove off with Randal behind the wheel. Riggs followed.

"Well, I've got to hand it to you," said Mabler, "you got through on the first try, but I can't be too thankful. It was you who started this whole mess, you and Ramseur. Even so, talking to her has eased my mind; I think we're going to work it out. Part two is you and Ramseur getting us a new home."

"I hadn't considered that," said Randal.

"You can start considering any time."

"I didn't mean—"

"We *had* us a nice place."

"The Graceland of trailers?" said Randal.

"You call it a double-wide once; then it is *home.*"

"Well, I'll bring it up with Mr. Ramseur, and we'll find you something," said Randal as they set off toward Round Wilson and its Christmas holiday spirit, followed out of town by the Grinch, a humorless Harlan Riggs who would soon deliver a most unwelcome present.

~ ~ ~

They wound their way up Mt. Gertrude's recently plowed switchbacks and when they entered the town, they noted something odd: there was a demonstration with protesters on the sidewalk waving placards. Randal recognized Jensen who was wearing a sign board with the PETPEv logo. He pulled into an empty space and with Mabler got out to view the scene, and Riggs also parked and then strolled over to window shop adjacent stores. Within moments, a car he recognized pulled up and the Reverend Tarbush got out wearing what Riggs saw was a toupee.

"I heard you were home from school Jen, but what is all this?" said the Rev.

"Feast your eyes, father, for they have sinned against the microcosm." Reverend Tarbush took in the signs: *Eat Nuts Not Gnats*; *Picket the Cricket*; *Free the Flea and Fly*; and *Address the Evils of Eating Weevils.*

"All living things are sacred."

"But you cannot do this, this display, it runs—"

"You have railed against these people for years, father, now is your chance! Join me in the regiment of the righteous and expel these merchants of the macabre from selling death here, but worse, they supply it in bulk to that cult on the hill."

Tarbush was conflicted. Yes, the store stood for much that he had taught himself to despise: free love and sex, mandalas and chanting and beads and feathers and toe rings and lava lamps, and all of it reeking of patchouli oil, but he needed this store, and no sooner had the thought passed when the door opened and the central object of that need stepped out.

"Jensen, this is just way un-cool," said Button. "I thought we cleared this up."

"As a death merchant you have no moral ground," he said, and led the chanting:

"*No moral ground! No moral ground! No moral ground! No moral ground!*"

A crowd had formed; itself a signal event in the sleepy town, but word quickly spread. Lurking nearby in a doorway a partially concealed Mabler spied someone he recognized, whereas the hooded parka, knit cap, and wraparound sunglasses he'd purchased in Ashville that afternoon masked him and he felt certain that he could pass unknown, and that was just as well, for here was an odd turn of events in a series of them.

"Son, I want you to go home now and help your mother trim the tree," stated Tarbush.

"My place, my place is here," said Jensen, "leading the righteous against the wicked." One of the wicked brought forth a garden hose and hooked it to the spigot on the side of the building.

"Disperse I say!" declared Button. Nobody paid her much attention.

"Move!" she yelled, but her voice was lost in the chanting.

"Let me handle this," said Randal, who shouted: "Get lost or get wet!" It got their attention and the closest backed away to stand behind their leader. With the afternoon temperature hovering in the thirties none of them welcomed a shower, none save Jensen who hoisted a finger and a placard in the other hand just as Button squeezed the handle and the blast of spray hit him in the face. He dropped the sign and ran with his troop at his heels, their placards left lying on the sidewalk like yesterday's ads.

"Such brisance is wholly uncalled for young lady," charged Tarbush, flustered and dripping. Button was stupified. She'd been so taken with the folly of the son that she hadn't noticed his presence.

"Well, I suppose the phrase, *like father, like son* would be an understatement," she said, but then caught herself from apologizing. Tarbush started to speak but then turned and strode to his car, muttering, vengeance will be mine, and quite oblivious to the bystanders that included his friend Harlan who stood rubbing his jaw, and who would soon be on his way back to Ashville.

It was clear to Riggs that Poe and the Springfield squaw were a Christmas duet, so it would be the perfect time to creep the boy's apartment, at least for starters. Maybe that would dislodge the shard of that nameless whatever that was nagging him. What was it? Something had moved a puzzle piece, maybe in that charade in front of Blue Jay Way. As he drove away, he couldn't put a finger on it, cough it up, or draw it out, and his thoughts shifted once again to the Springfield parents, Cody and Amanda. How had they gotten a daughter so different from either of them? Okay, the hair was maybe Cody, but neither parent was complected that way: the girl could pass for a full-blooded Cherokee. Is that the connection? No, that's the result of too many dives into the gene pool. He watched the road and concentrated on his driving, but it wouldn't come to him. Experience told him that it was a siren, the pealing of a distant bell just beyond the audible and he reviewed the confrontation from beginning to end, but it didn't help. He arrived in Ashville at dusk.

The street was deserted, and he climbed the stairs and slipped the jimmy bar between the door and the jamb and was inside in no more time than if he had used a key and then turned on a table lamp, figuring that Poe wasn't the type to inform his neighbors of vacation plans. On a table he recognized a book and picked it up and fanned the pages of *Ye Olde Granger Almanac*, with C. Springfield stamped on a slip of paper inserted in the slipcover. His pulse sped up when he found in the Table of Contents: *The Radiant Nebula of Winter Squash*, by R. B., and he stared off into the past, but when he refocused a moment later the kitchen wall map caught his eye with its colored pattern of pins and then he read the pages of Poe's notebook stuffed with news stories. Between the clippings and the longhand, a picture began to form. He said aloud: "Poe, you are dead meat."

"Excuse me?" Riggs spun to face a fat man in a charcoal Burberry standing in the open doorway.

"Who are you?" demanded Tarleton Ramseur.

As Riggs identified himself, he drew a folded sheet of paper from his jacket, waved it and put it back.

"Warrant," he said, as though that were enough.

"I'd like to see that."

"And just who is asking?"

"I am Tarleton Ramseur of the Ashville Mountain News. I must say, I am deeply concerned. What exactly has Poe done to confer on him a B and E?"

Riggs considered. Anybody else he would have abused, but the press, for Christ's sake! "Your colleague is withholding evidence in a federal investigation, but it's no surprise given his criminal past." Ramseur parried.

"If you're referring to the incident of the swine, I would hardly call that act recidivist. Do tell me, what is this investigation? Start with particulars." He hoped the agent would enlarge on Randal's thumb print already gained from a previous evening in this room, as well as snippets he had garnered on his own.

"I am not at liberty to say, but if you want to help your friend, get him a lawyer."

"What do you intend to charge him with?"

"He's a material witness to a string of armed robberies," said Riggs.

"I think you're on shaky ground," said Ramseur. Riggs shoved his face within an inch from Ramseur's.

"If you interfere, I'll have your ass too!" and with that he barged out the door. Ramseur picked up a vase, but then thought better of it. Why ruin a vase?

2

Together, Randal and Button dropped off Mabler at the ridge top wire and then headed down the other side. They had traded Randal's car for an old Willys Jeep, on loan from Jam, and they took the switchbacks with ease. Snow began to dance in their headlights as they drove into the parking area in front of the post and beam onetime park headquarters, smoke charging out of the stone chimney, and moments later they stood in front of its massive river stone hearth warming their hands once Ruth, bundled in a red and purple checked cardigan, had ushered them inside.

"Well, my children of the night, what stories have you?"

"Magical, madcap or mundane, which would you prefer?" replied Button, as Randal surveyed the great room with its exposed beams and yellowed knotty pine walls lined with bookshelves and photographs. A pool table in one corner was covered with books and papers.

"You know me child, you just run away with it while I get us some tea."

Button made up a tale in iambs about how each voice in the mountain was controlled by a whisper or an echo of steam that for centuries had no other release than singing, and annually at Christmas the voices rose to a crescendo that could only be compared to Handel's Messiah.

Randal again measured the width of his lust as equal to Button's sublime brilliance that plumbed depths in extemporaneous presentation, and he fell in love all over again.

They huddled on a loveseat before a double pane picture window alive with snowfall, coming heavier now. Ruth served them tea and sat opposite beneath an antler rack hung with hats.

"That was just lovely dear; it is our mountain, is it not? Okay, now, what's all this about progressive politics downtown?"

"What did you hear?" said Button.

"Now dear, don't fall into the habit of answering a question with a question, you'll end up a news reporter," said Ruth, and winked at Randal. "We'll let him do his job: report."

"Well, ah, this fellow we know who heads up the campus chapter of an insect rights group and, as it so happens—"

"Now don't digress, Mr. Poe. We'll never be friends," said Ruth.

"He's your Reverend Tarbush's son."

"Indeed. Old brimstone's younger spawn I haven't seen much of—his daughter, you should know, is doing graduate work at the Sorbonne. Now what's that allegory about first born, blue blood?" said Ruth.

"He has a moral conflict with the sale of edible bugs," said Randal. Button nudged him.

"Well, in my experience, an overburdened morality will drive anyone bugs, said Ruth. "*That* is the conflict. So, let me guess. Home for the holidays, he zeroes in on Blue Jay Way."

"The true conflict is that he and I had a—a fling, just a brief encounter, and he took it to be, well, you know how boys are," said Button.

"Wait a second," said Randal.

"She means the locals, don't you dear? Their grasp of romance is limited to crop rotation."

Randal seethed a bit over Button's flippant remark and the tailing of Ruth's follow through, but it passed as quickly as it had come.

"The sheriff was at the checkout desk when the call came in," said Ruth.

"Is he still after you?" said Button

"He's a puppy chasing his tail," said Ruth. "I have long suspected that he is after something else entirely, but a little sweet talk goes a long way at my age. Now, if our handsome young reporter will abide, we have some clothing to discuss," and with that the two women went upstairs.

Randal took his cup to the sink and was perusing knickknacks when his cell phone beeped. The text from Tarleton warned of Riggs and advised him to stay away from his apartment. The women came back down.

"I will hem it tonight, dear, and you can pick it up tomorrow. Then we'll go and give our darling Gertrude her Christmas present," said Ruth. "Before you go, Mr. Poe, drag that tree in off the back porch and set it in the stand, I can handle the rest of it."

Back in the Jeep they kissed and held each other as the heater warmed up, and then headed up through the heavy fall and accumulated drifts toward Rainbow Run and Jam's lauded hot hard apple cider, a drink that for Randal would be memorable.

3

Dr. Argon Kyrkcops dismissed his sycophant train and when they had scattered and all was still, he paced beneath the glass dome of the celestial center, and the movement helped to keep him focused; his office had too many distractions, not the least of which was his new secretary who seemed just a tad too nosy for her station. Things had to be sorted out before they became too complicated and a solution unattainable. It was time to draw in the reigns and prepare for the ultimate departure: Nibiru, as was proclaimed in the Cydonian Scrolls. But there could be no interference, no dangling tentacles of requirements, nor tripwires of unfinished business.

The first order was cohorts. They had to be brought in, perhaps piecemeal, with the greatest care and then sequestered together, and away from the body of Mystic Knights. They were not of this or any social group and could be disruptive when allowed to roam free, as had proven the case with one. Well, he *had* gotten careless and that kind of behavior had but a single therapist: John Law. It had been the first ever crack in a system he knew to be flawless, and therefore the timing for the departure would arrive none too soon, before that crack widened into a fissure. Where he would put them, he wasn't sure. Think!

Then, there was that other matter of the Iconic Transcendent Symbols, the Beacons of which the Scrolls prophesied and without which the transferable liftoff could not be made: The Earth Mother and a Righteous King; the scrolls failed to specify precisely in that regard, but he had one that surely would suffice, and would snare the other soon. They too would need to be sequestered, but for that he had just the place. It was priceless, really: a pint-sized granite-walled grotto, an oubliette just below where he paced.

Finally, there was Mrs. Nungesser who was quite simply too large for the rocket ship; her weight alone would embrace gravity and thus keep them all earthbound. Besides, he doubted she could fit through the hatch, and pictured the ghastly image of her stuck halfway and hanging an awful moon as the precious moment elapsed. This was indeed the biggest challenge: could she read his thoughts, and might she even now be planning some rupture? But that was rash; he well knew she could only mind-read and entrance her subjects when in direct line of sight contact, and only in that identity. Keep her entranced and on the oblique, he cautioned, but he had been slipping lately, randomly losing control, and he had pegged it to lust; when he got his rocks off, his guard seemingly melted away and all within his spherical domain slipped from the elliptical. He had pondered the paradox before: he drew power from the mesmerized, and his words held them placid as lambs beside still waters, and in turn that energy lifted others to his bidding, that is, until his own clarion call to submission and worship admitted of another voice crying to be heard, another personality sharing the strength. Was that unraveling him? But getting back to matters at hand, he concluded that a meeting with his Sergeant-at-arms and the security detail was the first step; they must be led to believe a threat loomed in the person of Mrs. Nungesser, one that must be acted on with stealth.

~ ~ ~

In his room Mabler was making plans of his own. He had stowed his various non-Elvis disguises in a pillowcase tied with a shoelace. The following night when, as the Granger's Almanac assured him, there would be no moon, he would go over the fence where he knew the razor wire to be plastic realia placed there by his host, whom he judged to be a clown of many faces, cheapskate being the least among them. On the one hand he was impressed, from the standpoint of one adept at the visual subterfuge of disguise, with his host's duality: when you dealt with one of him you never saw the other; on the other hand, he was revolted by that very duplicity. But how could that be? Wasn't he a living example of the very thing that now repulsed him? Was it professional jealousy, perhaps? He'd lived a double life for many years: Elvis by night and Delray at any other time, so what was it that rubbed him the wrong way? Maybe it was Poe again, whom he had almost forgiven. It was the kid who had told him of the bank heists and showed him the evidence, such as it was, of Argon's purported involvement. The documentation and news stories made an impression that fit with his own misgivings about his host and these surroundings, and so he had not questioned it. He believed it because he wanted, needed to make sense of things within his own world that so recently had been turned inside out. But it still bugged him; Poe could have it all wrong and maybe he did, but if that was the case, did it explain Argon's presence at the demonstration?

Well, it didn't much matter. His wife and son were already on their way to Ashville where they would reconcile and be reunited and hammer it together once more with the desire and the will to go on, to live their lives together as planned, just like any family, wouldn't they? Reclining, he opened Argon's opus to Volume III, and yawned.

~ ~ ~

In another wing of the compound, Mrs. Nungesser came out of the trance state and knew without looking that she was *there* once again, the very place in which she had repeatedly *come to*, as it were, and now, once again, she shuddered, and by rote removed her costume and looked about for her clothes. What was she going to tell her husband when she finally found the nerve to broach the topic, one she had thus far been utterly unable to assemble? Then, as she pulled on her Danskins, she felt herself slipping again into a bluish spectrum and radiant whorl and the next thing she noted was the pile of peeled carrots in her colander in the kitchen sink, and she washed them with her tears as she remembered the wire maze.

4

Randal eyed Button across the room in a huddle of women as he sidled up to Jam. They stood awhile without speaking as a fiddle and mandolin dueled in a corner and the tide of party conversation rose and fell as though each were an uncertain accompanist.

"What is in this, anyway? said Randal.

"Apples, can't you tell?"

"I should a known better. Apples don't have kick."

"You might be surprised."

"Well, I would be, wouldn't I?" said Randal, as Cody sidled up.

"Is our Mr. Jeffries treatin' you alright?"

"Like Newton, an apple hit him on the head."

"Yes, and myself likewise, followed by a great idea," said Cody. He pulled a Golden Delicious from his coat and held it up to Randal's nose. "Would you care to partake?"

"As long as it won't sap my energy," said Randal.

"Not to worry, why, it will put a twinkle in the apple of your eye."

"We haven't really talked about it, are you sure she's cool with me doing this," said Randal as he lit the pipe.

"When the day dawns that girl of mine isn't cool about something, well, you could see it from year one, she redefined the term," said Cody.

"'Like a true nature's child, she was born, born to be wild,'" said Jam, and topped off their mugs of cider.

Randal felt a great ease settle into him trailing a joy that made little things funny and funny things funnier and he traded jabs with Cody and Jam as they shared the bowl and the cider also went around and around.

It was still going around when Randal awoke the next morning, or was it the loft and mandala that spun? He lay still and quiet for a while until he reached for the water on the nightstand and found himself alone. He started to get up, thought better of it, and dozed off. Later, as he helped himself to breakfast downstairs, thankful for the coffee already made and the trays of fruit and pastry, he knew he had missed once again a chance to meet the fabled Gertrude the Bear, after reading Button's note pinned to an apple.

Stepping out on the porch to clear his head he narrowly missed assassination by snowball. After thirty minutes of packing, throwing, dodging, and ducking, what hangover remained was threadbare in the wardrobe of consciousness, and he offered to help Jam move some crates to Blue Jay Way.

The streets were silent in the snow-muffled town save for the rattling of the tire chains, and so both men were startled by the bloop of a siren as they approached the store. Jam stopped in the empty street.

"Good morning, Jeffries," said Sheriff Roberts, "sorry to bother you at this hour."

"Sup?"

"I have a warrant here for the arrest of one Randal Poe, that one, am I correct?"

"What in hell, Bob. Tomorrow is Christmas!"

"Just doing my job, you know how it is, and while we're at it, the county's snowplow, you know, that old International, froze up yesterday, think you can take a look at it?"

"I won't do squat until you tell me what's up."

"Well, it seems that he's wanted by the F.B.I. in connection to some bank holdups." Jam couldn't swallow it and did his best, but to no avail. Randal filled him in on Riggs and asked him to call Tarleton Ramseur.

"A couple phone calls Randal and you'll be out in time for lunch."

"What will we have, snowball stew?" said Randal as he was handcuffed.

"You got it, man."

At the station, Randal was fingerprinted, the ink pad and jailer's hands icy cold in the slate grey room, and he was then led to one of three cells by the same cheerless employee. He sat on the bunk as the cell door clanged shut and despite his efforts to rekindle the flair of nonchalance that he and Jam had used with the Sheriff, it couldn't be relit; the spark was gone, and all that remained in its place was the snoring of a vomit-stained Santa two cells down.

Several hours later Jam and Cody were ushered into the cell block and Randal leaped to the bars to shake hands but the looks they gave him were grave. Cody looked murderous.

"Guys, what is it? I'm getting out of here, right?"

"Randal," Jam said, "Button has disappeared!"

"Disapp—what do you mean?"

"Randal, you look me in the eye, you swear you had no hand in this," said Cody.

"Hand in what? She's gone? What's going on?"

Cody strode from the cellblock and Jam rested his arms on the bars.

"The Jeep was found down near Ruth's, out in the road, engine running, the driver's door open, CDs and other stuff scattered around. She fought like a lion; I know that much. We're looking everywhere. Everybody's out looking, but it's bad, man. This kind of shit doesn't happen."

"Jam, it has got to be Riggs. He's got me in here; she's in another jail maybe? Check it out!"

"This is some funky voodoo, man. Somebody broke into Blue Jay Way too and stole all the crystals and gemstones. Left a trail of bug food in the snow."

"Can you get me out of here? I didn't do anything but piss off that Fed, Riggs."

"Randal, whatever it is, they got your bail so high a rocket couldn't get there. I'm sorry man, but with all this shit goin' down, you're gonna have to chill, you know?"

But after Jam left, he didn't chill at all as he raked his memory for anything that might have been a tip off, a clue of some sort and he reviewed their recent mealtime conversations, their rollicking banter, even their intimate moments, but he came up empty. There didn't seem to be anything at all in the way of a wrinkle in a lifestyle as smooth as glass, except for her confrontation with Jensen on the campus and then again at the store. Was he involved? It didn't seem possible; picketing a store is one thing, but kidnapping? Or could it be the case of a jilted lover gone around the bend? He reflected on his own ruined love affair at Hogville and then of Elmer's bitterness over his brother and of Eddie Terrell's romantic thievery, but neither had precipitated violence. He mulled and worried until the jailer came to tell him he'd be allowed one phone call, but he knew the routine, having been processed through the system for his swindle of the history museum and the theft of a thousand head of experimental swine. He got through to Carolotta on the first ring, figuring her a surer bet than her husband who was often not at his desk and who had the unerring habit of keeping his cell phone turned off.

As the deputy closed the door Randal had his glimmer of hope doused with the news that the Round Wilson magistrate's office would be closed for the holidays and thereby unable to process bail bonds until after the New Year. He sat on the bunk, hung his head and said a prayer for Button.

~ ~ ~

He awoke the following morning with the opening of the cell door, but instead of Ramseur and the relief he would have brought it was none other than Harlan Riggs followed by a Deputy with a card table and two folding chairs. Randal leered.

"Your buddy Welch has got the Hilton compared to this," said Riggs.

Randal said nothing, figuring, why bother?

"We're going to have us a set to, the two of us, just you and me," said Riggs, seating himself.

"Where are you holding Button, and why! She's got *nothing* whatever to do with Welch or anything else!"

A light shone in Riggs' eyes. In his briefing with the sheriff, he had learned of the girl's disappearance.

"Sit down here and we'll talk," said Riggs.

"You tell me where she is!"

"Son, you put your ass in that chair or I will."

Reluctantly, Randal sat and faced the agent.

"I'll all but hand you your hot little Indian squeeze, but first you start from the beginning, with your first visit to Welch." He set a digital recorder on the table between them, and soon Randal recounted the interviews and what they had exchanged and why he had begun to dig a little deeper into the bank heists.

"Okay, so the Beige Aryans gang headed east. What was the reason?" asked Riggs.

"They were no longer the BA, they'd changed their name, and then adopted a new identity to escape from their parent organization," said Randal.

"Yeah, we know. B.U.T.T hasn't kept their butts below the radar." said Riggs. Randal was sure that Welch hadn't told the agent anything other than what he should do to himself, now a shared sentiment. How could Riggs have known? The agent read the question in his face.

"We had the interrogation room bugged, but not until the two of you had become pals."

"I am not his friend."

"You put a guy like that in print, glorify him, he's not a buddy? Bullshit."

"Riggs, you've said it as much yourself, he's got nothing you want to hear. You want to get something, you have to trade. I traded, and what I got was—wait a second! You said *bugged*?"

"More commonly called a wiretap, court order, the whole works," said Riggs.

"It's the bugs!" said Randal.

"Make sense Poe, I don't have all day."

"No, that's it, that's the axel on the wheel. I've got a wall map where I—"

"We've got your map, your whole set up."

"You people broke into my—you are fucking unbelievable!"

"Believe this Poe, you open up or I will shut you down for good."

"You got *my* map, I am surprised, no, amazed that you don't have one of your own. The robberies form a ring around a three-state area all about a hundred miles out from the center of that wheel. Want me to tell you where the center is, or would you prefer to deduce it?"

"Don't be a smartass, kid. I'm the one asking the questions."

"Just a glance will tell you, but I used a protractor, and nearly dead center on that compass is none other than Round Wilson, but that's not all."

"Let it roll kid, you're doing great."

"Button first. If I learned anything at all from Harvey Welch, this is it."

"You sonofabitch, you don't have any idea who you're dealing with!"

"Just tell me where she is."

Riggs considered his hole card and concluded that he was close enough to the real jackpot that it wasn't worth the gamble.

"She is not in custody. I don't have her. The Sheriff has the whole county out beating the bushes, and in this weather, that is something."

Randal glanced at the cell door.

"Don't even think about it, Poe. But I'll do what I can if you level with me."

"No, you won't; you lied about her. I need to be out there as well, but you're going to keep me in here even after I give you every little tidbit, because that's the kind of man you are. Besides, a town this size, the magistrate is gone, who wouldn't be at Christmas?!"

"You think I am without feelings for your lady friend, but you are wrong. What you don't understand is the time that has gone into this investigation; we have been looking for these creeps for a long, long time and I have to say it, thanks to you we are closer than we've ever been, perhaps closer than we know. Give me the rest of it and I'll get that magistrate out of his fart sack at midnight." Randal seethed, but then let go.

"Well, the gang's been going out from Round Wilson to rob banks to get the funds needed for another group they're in cahoots with. This is conjecture, but it adds up, and here's why: Better Us Than Them has a contract, if that's what you'd call it, to deliver one-hundred tons of micro-livestock to the cult—you know about them?" Riggs waved a hand for him to go on.

"Well, they have a rocket and they're planning a mission into space, apparently," said Randal.

"Where they will dine on bugs?"

"I know, it sounds fantastic, but insects are not all that weird. You can find them in the recipe and menu books of some fine metropolitan restaurants. According to Welch, you can bake a pan of honeybees at a low temperature for eight hours or so and then sift them into flour. But the big picture suggests that if we ate more insects, then we would use less pesticide."

"But not in outer space," said Riggs.

"Yeah, but anyway the local connection is Blue Jay Way. A large chunk of that purchase order is coming through the store. Cody and his family only collected rent from the cult until they were contracted to supply them with the edible cuisine; you can be sure that they are not part of that other business. Their store is a convenient channel, that's all."

"Alright, I'll give you this much: they are not under suspicion in any real sense, although I'd like to have a nice heart to heart chat with Cody sometime, go over old ground, see if we turn up anyone we know in common."

Randal was about to say that Cody didn't like cops, but caught himself: what would it matter in the face of things?

"You said the gang *goes out* from here. What do you know about that?"

Randal thought of Jam's remark about cult members changing clothes in the road, and Ruth's info about the abandoned car together with what Mabler had told him on their way back to Round Wilson from the teleconference, as well as his networking with regional editors and reporters. As he was forming his answer a sudden commotion stole his attention, and that of his interrogator, for just then Tarleton Ramseur and another man stormed down the corridor and into the open cell, trailed by a gesticulating deputy.

"Don't say another word, Randal," said Tarleton, whose overcoat heaved with his exertion.

"What is the meaning of this? Deputy, escort these men out of here," said Riggs.

"Now hold on, sir. I am C. Dalton Pembroke, attorney for the Mountain News, and I have here a writ commanding the cessation of this interview, and in so doing freeing Mr. Poe on my employer's recognizance." Riggs snapped the paper from the lawyer's hand and read it. Glaring, he picked up his recorder, told Randal they were not finished, and stalked out.

"Now that's what you might call the power of the press," said Tarleton, "and on Christmas day no less."

Randal questioned them about Button, but there was no news. He thanked them both when they dropped him off at the foot of the road up to Rainbow Run, but Tarleton also climbed from the car and held up a pair of snowshoes:

"A friend in need is a friend in deed." They trudged up into the snow together.

5

The Tarbush family gathered around the speaker phone and chatted with their daughter in France, inquiring after her health and studies and other interests and wishing her the best for Christmas. Then they headed for the dining room where a golden turkey centerpiece graced an elaborate table. They said grace, and then dug in and their chatter trailed off into the inarticulate language of mastication, interrupted by an occasional request for more. As the Reverend ate, he sought to imagine the tables turned and Button spread-eagled on buffalo hide, when Millicent raised her eyes from the plate and dropped her fork and arose, arms dead at her sides, and walked from the table and into the kitchen where she collided with the refrigerator. The Reverend sprang to his feet and guided her back to the table, whispering in her ear what sounded to a stunned Jensen like a kind of buzzing, a repetitive mumble with a refrain that slithered from his father as though he was speaking in tongues as he sat her back down and tucked in her napkin before reseating himself.

"Mom, are you okay?"

"She's fine, son. She's been having these spells lately. It's nothing serious." Jensen wasn't convinced and asked her again. What he heard instead startled them both.

"The final larvae consignment … will arrive in a fortnight," she droned.

"What!? Mom, what are you—"

"This will yield a net weight of two thousand two hundred and thirty-six pounds, four shy of the total due to shifting: *grubs, moths, wasps, and cicadas, beetles, foood; grubs, moths, wasps and cicadas, beetles, foood; grubs, moths, wasps, and cicadas, beetles, foood* she intoned in French accented English. Both men shot out of their chairs, jabbering like apes, the father drawing her one way and the son the other, but hey got her to the sofa and her husband ran from the room. Jensen heard the back door slam as he caressed his mother's hand and stroked her brow, and he had a vision then that the devil had entered his home, and he was pretty sure he knew its source: it was Button who'd told him in her wicked way that they were buying bulk for the cult on the hill. How all that evil got into his mother wasn't hard to figure. As he tended to her, he knew he wasn't the first convert, rather he had followed her unconscious bidding to rid the world of micro murderers and he had done so as would any son true to his mother's desire. She slumbered then, and he went to talk to his father, but the reverend was nowhere to be seen, although his tracks were visible in the snow. Why had he run into the woods? Jensen returned to the house and called the family doctor to attend to his mom and said he'd leave the door open. Once the doctor arrived, he donned his parka and set out across the yard following the still visible impressions made by his father's mad dash from the house, but the footsteps gave out not far into the woods at the foot of a granite outcrop. He scanned the area but saw no more prints. What in this world? Soon his own footprints confused the scene and he returned to the house in time to see the doctor off. Assured that his mother was safe in the good hands of sedation, he assured the doctor that he would return soon and begged a ride into town to be dropped off at the Dairy Queen which he knew to be a crow fly mile from the cult compound. That it was all uphill and twenty-five degrees didn't matter, for he was charged with righteousness and armed with the certainty of his and his mother's beliefs.

Before he was aware that he had traversed the distance, he found an unguarded gatepost and the way wide open and went in the main door and down a hallway and into the first door that caught his eye and what next caught his eye stopped him in his tracks.

"Seize that man!" cried Kyrkcops, as he and his lieutenants looked over a map. Jensen was bundled into plastic ligatures and gagged and stuffed into a closet by six bald and beefy men. After what seemed an eternity, he was duck walked to another room, down a flight of steps, and trundled into a pitch-dark space that smelled of loam. As he fell, he thought of his mother and prayed that she would deliver him from evil when his head struck hard and a flash of blazing amber was all he knew.

~ ~ ~

A few snowy miles away, Harlan Riggs stewed. Where had the lawyer obtained a writ on Christmas day? He had no such network and would need to drive down to Ashville just to chase up a federal judge. What rotten timing. He was so close he sensed he could smell the bandit's skunk oil aftershave, so again he turned to his computer files and reviewed what he had. Was there something he had missed? You read your own writing long enough you fail to notice glitches. He forced himself to go methodically one line at a time but by the time he'd come to the end his eyes ached and he was no closer than before. His thoughts trailed off to the Springfield daughter and the sheriff's comments. 'Bob Robert sure had his hands full now. It'll be interesting to see how the backcountry Sheriff handles this, he'll probably deputize half the county.' He then reviewed the jail interview and went over what Poe had told him about the AB offshoot becoming the Beige Aryans and then their cross-country travels that had brought them finally to—hang on a minute! Now, what is the name of that group up there; got it here somewhere: Mystic Knights of Moonstone Light. Yeah, and *that is it, isn't it*, been gnawing at me for weeks! Moonstone is what color? It's Beige. Beige! Harlan Riggs strapped on his shoulder holster, checked the clip and then strapped a backup piece to his calf. Leaving an urgent message with the dispatcher he ran to his truck and drove away.

~ ~ ~

The gathering was a large one and some of them were still milling on the porch stomping the snow off their boots as Ruth brought extra chairs and blankets and then bent to stoke the fire in the woodstove. When all were in and settled, they went over what they'd done and which sectors had been covered. From the get go, Ruth had organized the town and set them forth on a grid pattern using the old Forest Service maps left by her husband.

"Thing is, we just don't have enough people to adequately cover the area," said one.

"Well, we got our kids out there, neighbors and what all," said another.

"Even a few outsiders, I notice," said a third, nodding at Tarleton and Randal who sat side by side nursing hot ciders.

"What we need are some bloodhounds, but old Bobby Rob got none."

"Shoot, he did they'd be fat as he is."

"Can bloodhounds work in snow? You never see it on TV, like you can escape only in summer." And on it went, but the latter remark jolted Ruth out of the funk that had set her organizational abilities fluttering but otherwise blocked out what the possible might entail. Now, her sense was as though she had awakened from a daydream.

"Hey! Listen up! We have a bloodhound better than any dog! Why I never thought of it before is a fright! We've been out there now too long without her. Gertrude knows this area like the back of her paw and better still, she knows the girl just as well. All we need is some item of clothing that Button wore recently. Randal, can you help?"

"I can get something from Rainbow Run, surely. Cody and Jam and the rest will rendezvous here in an hour, but I'll go now," he said.

"I'll drive you," said Lou-Ann Strayhorn, "then I got to go to work. But I aim to stick by the radio no matter what."

Randal was back in thirty minutes with a toboggan and a shirt and the party swarmed out of doors again and waited in the parking lot. Ruth came into view leading Gertrude who was seen to dance about, unaware of her solemn duty. The groups split up and Ruth and bear were joined by Randal and Tarelton and followed shortly after by Jam and Cody and Amanda who had arrived piled onto a snowmobile. They huddled as the bear sniffed the garments and then they set off, heading up the side of the mountain that shared the name of the bear. Cody hiked at the back and Randal filled him in on what he suspected about Jensen, as it was the only thing that made any sense. Randal could see that Cody was torn by the news as he pulled Jam aside, and then the lanky mechanic went back down the hill as the search party continued upward. An hour later they paused in a clearing Randal recognized even though there had been no snow on the ground his last time; here were the berry bushes and the tree with the burl beneath the forked trunk. Gertrude recognized something as well and she rooted about with her nose in the ground and when underbrush was tossed to the side, they all saw it: a cave. Gertrude was wagging her big head and mewling as she shuffled in, and disappeared. One by one they followed her in and up they went like the spellbound children of Hamelin.

6

The object of their concern paced in a narrow windowless room and worried about her mom and dad and Jam and Peaches and everybody on the farm and Randal too and what they would think and where they might be, and between these thoughts flashed signals of anger and disbelief and fear in no pattern whatever and she couldn't take it all sitting down.

She tried the door again, knowing it would be locked, and put her ear to the panel also knowing she would hear nothing. The only thing she knew with any degree of certainty was that against her will she was trapped in a windowless concrete rectangle, a storeroom that held cartons of costumes for men and women and Halloween masks and Mylar unisex bodysuits, and that she had been overpowered and dragged from her Jeep by two big men with bald heads. Chrome Cretins, she said aloud, and noted that her voice was calm. She recalled her fight when they came for her: she had kneed one of them and given the other a bloody nose before they had gotten the upper hand. She spoke aloud again and recited a poem, and it calmed her down enough to do some Yoga and breathing exercises. Then she remembered her lucky crystal and dug it from her watch pocket and set it beside her. Deep into the breathing she knew she would have a visitor and within a meditative moment the lock clicked and in stepped a man she knew.

"The Earth Mother has arrived at last. This is a great day for the Mystic Knights," said Argon Kyrkcops. "You will join me for dinner with the King."

"You will never get away with this. You will go to jail. Now let me out of here!"

"Your presence among us is prophesied; this is your destiny, and it is a great—" and Button tore past him and into the corridor but found it sealed. She turned on her heel and raced to the other end but found no exit there either. He came out of nowhere, she thought, as she leaned in the doorway.

He turned toward her and smiled before walking through what had been a concrete wall but was now a fissure that led to a short flight of stairs, and up he went.

She hesitated before following, and then not too closely, for while he was unmistakably the Reverend Tarbush in the face, everything else seemed wrong.

Stepping through an archway she knew in an instant she was in the anteroom to the dome from its curvilinear walls to the expansive ceiling and its refracted light, memories flashed of playing there; dancing the frog with her mom and dad and hopping with Mr. Jiggs and planting secrets and talisman in rafter nooks and under creaky floorboards, but encountering an Elvis Presley here was certainly a first. She took a step toward the oval wooden table at which he reposed in his fringed white leather suit, watching her. Argon then stepped into her vision and invited her to sit but only did so when her host preceded her. He spoke:

"It is my deep and heartfelt honor to introduce the Earth Mother and a Righteous King; the presence of both has been prophesied so it is only natural and fitting that you are here among the brethren and sistren."

Looking closely while noting that *sistren* was not a word, Button saw that the King was none other than Mr. Mabler who appeared to be asleep with his eyes open. She focused on remembering where those nooks and floorboards were located as a recessed Lazy Susan rose in the center of the table like an oval leaf, and on it sat a hunk of quartz. The Reverend double snapped his fingers and as Mabler awoke their host warmed to his preamble.

"Crystals are bridges of light into the memories of ancient knowledge we all carry within, inscribed in our souls, that connect us to our intergalactic origins through the coded language of gemstones and into the crystalline properties of the transitional magnetic field of..." Button tuned him out and focused on a glum Mr. Mabler but got his attention with her foot, and then through facial gestures and hand signals tried to communicate but quickly saw that wasn't going to get it ..."and in this new age these power centers will be granted an homage undue their celestial—" Button slapped the tabletop.

"Hey Rev, save it, I need to talk to my friend, here."

Kyrkcops glared at her, popeyed, as though the interruption had speared him. He got to his feet, bowed, and left the room.

"Ms. Springfield, what is going on here, can you tell me?" gasped Mabler.

"How long have you been here—the dome?"

"Well, it's a bit fuzzy, but I think our host is insane." He filled her in on his discoveries about the Mystic Knights' so-called prophecies, the congregants, and their presumed roles.

"You've got to be kidding!"

"He believes me to be the Real McCoy and you a native goddess, and that he—"

"He's a Baptist minister in a bald toupee." It was her turn to explain, but she didn't know where to begin.

"Ms. Springfield, I believe we're in danger, but more so you, as he intends, well, how does one say it?"

"Just say it, Del."

"Okay, well, you're to be a sacrifice on the altar of the landing platform, and I am supposed to, well, wield the scepter or something. He makes me do things against my will, him and that hippodrome harridan. I see I am confusing you, but we need to get *out* of here," and at that moment she remembered and scurried over to find the niche in the panel, one of the hidden crawl spaces left by Jam and Cody when they built the structure. It was still there but it wasn't going to fit them both, having been designed for a child. In less than a minute she had arranged him in the least contorted position they could negotiate and then got herself reseated at the table when Kyrkcops returned. He stopped halfway in the door.

"That is odd, very odd indeed," he said.

"What is, Rev?" she said and offered up the smile that always melted him.

"You won't be smiling long, my little pretty. Now, where is the king? There is only one way out of this room."

He turned on his heel and spoke with the guard at the door. Button took the initiative and strode up to them both, but before she reached the doorway, felt herself veering off as though pulled by an invisible wave and though she resisted and won for a moment her body then veered backward against her will and soon she was standing at the niche that exposed a narrow band of white leather fringe, and soon Mabler stood beside her, their backs flat against the wall as though hung there on clothes pegs.

"Well, I must say that I did not expect the two of you to get along, being from such distant and disparate echelon of the galaxy, and I surmised that there might be some difficulties as would befit the likes of powerful entities, but now I see that I must even sequester deities, and so it shall be." And he clapped his hands thrice.

7

Jam arrived at the Tarbush home on horseback and he was coming up the drive when he spied Mrs. Tarbush step out of a side door and head across the yard. She looked to be naked but when he drew closer saw that she wore a sheer nightie and heavy rubber boots, and he called to her, but she went on across the yard and into the trees. It was much too cold. Anybody strolls around in their underwear this time of year needs to be cared for. He forgot about the kid and the horse and went after her and when he entered the trees she was nowhere in sight, but her tracks led to the base of an outcrop and he caught a whiff of perfume and then a boot as it slipped between the rocks. He climbed up and followed, concerned for her health and safety, and discovered a fissure in the rock face that opened into a yawning cave. He called out to her again as he followed her perfume until the light from the mouth had dissipated and then fished his headlamp out of his pack. They were going upward.

~ ~ ~

"We might have to hoof it up their road after that ice last night," said Sheriff Weston.

Riggs nodded. "I'd say with what we've got it's a sure bet. If not, at least we can talk to them and maybe pick up a lead. And then there's your B and E." Roberts nodded.

Blue Jay Way had been broken into and goods taken. His report was incomplete and he hated disarray as much as any crime in his town; there was seldom much of either and he wanted to keep it that way, and he outlined what he had: the Springfield kid had vanished and apparently so had the Tarbush boy, both of whom were connected with the store; young Tarbush had argued with the girl on several occasions and then had picketed her store (without a permit, mind you); his Deputies were engaged in the search parties. He nodded again, put his pipe and tobacco in his pockets and led Riggs out of the office.

They headed out of town and up the mountain in four-wheel drive and made good time, considering. He made a radio check with his deputies and couldn't raise Lou-Ann but otherwise got no updates. He tried her again. Now that old girl knows her job as good as anybody and she hasn't checked in. We're headed to the right place: that's where she's supposed to be at. The foot of the road was slick and as it rose and angled, they slipped and slid until they nearly fishtailed into a gully. Roberts backed down and parked, unclamped the shotgun from its mount between the seats, and followed Riggs on foot up the frosty lane.

8

"Who's there?" The space was chill on her skin and her bare feet felt the earth, but otherwise she sat still and peered into the midnight ink. She called out again.

"It's Del, Ms. Springfield. They took my clothes; I'm naked as a Jaybird."

"You too, huh? Well, it's nature time all the time, I always say," but she didn't feel at all cocky.

"Any idea where we are?" he said.

"We're underground, that much I know, but my hands are tied, and I can only feel what's behind me," she said, and controlled another tremble arcing up from her belly. "We're a couple of trussed chickens, looks like." She had tied up the Reverend on many occasions, but they had always played with a safe word and a prearranged set of rules, and now he had returned the favor, it seemed, minus any rules at all. She had come *awake* without a memory of sleep—the last thing she recalled was opening the niche where she had hidden Mr. Mabler—and found herself thus. Not at all cool! She wriggled against the bonds, but they were very tight on her wrists, and then fought down the rising fear with a sense that she was right at home, an earth child in the womb of my mother and we are going to storm some badass lightening up your dirt-chute, preacher man!

"Del, can you make your way over here, just come toward my voice and keep moving this way until you are over here, that's you, okay, okay." They bumped again.

"Alright, we are going to stand back-to-back. Shuffle around now and you untie my wrists, and then I'll do yours, got it?"

She felt him against her and his fingers like spiders on her butt as he adjusted his stance. Well, she thought, chalk up another experience in the wild world of sex: cave bondage with a naked fake Elvis. Amanda can't top this one.

"I can't figure this thing out, like if there is a knot. There has to be a knot," he said.

"No, there isn't one. I can feel your wrists and it isn't rope. They're what cops use for riots when they round up crowds. We need a sharp rock and a lot of patience. Let's find a wall, and then you go one way and I'll go the other. You just let me know where you are so we don't get too separated; we don't know how big this cavern is." Their voices grew apart as a shiver passed through her.

"Don't get too far," he said.

"Del, maybe you should sing a song; Jailhouse Rock seems appropriate."

"I am surprised that one so young would even know it."

"Randal and my dad told me some and I Googled the rest," she said, "but it seems like you could shift up and cover someone more recent."

Her head bumped and she ducked and sidling further bumped again and then hunkered lower and as she did, she sensed a dampness brush her feet and she squatted, but it wasn't moisture, rather a whisper of air. She crabbed on slowly as Mabler began singing and she sensed the floor beginning to slope and as she moved downward the whisper grew in ghostly caresses on her flesh but then she whacked her left knee and ceased all movement as she fought a maelstrom of rage against Tarbush for this crass injustice and the pain in her leg that throbbed a tom-tom to yellow flashes and the coldness crawling in her belly and inching up her spine, a swirling menace to her dearest dreams and deep set love of loves but she grasped at love and held it then and wielded love and fought back and got around it all; and then after groping alternately with feet and hands determined her enemy to be an outcrop. She was about to call out when her foot nudged a soft object and she painfully knelt to gingerly fondle about the object, and only then did she yell. When Mabler arrived, they both spoke about the chillier air while they continued their investigation, and concluded that they had found a jagged rock face and beneath it the body of a fully clothed male.

"I can't detect a breath," said Mabler, but I cannot get angled in there right."

"This is really bad! This is just freaking me," her voice choking, as she sawed her wrists madly at the rock face, struggling to keep her arms free of its jagged surface. Her bloodless wrists and hands ached with cold.

"Hang on, I have something," said Mabler. "It feels like maybe a pocketknife.

She stopped and choked back tears and soon was squatting backwards beside him then and awkwardly they kneaded the object up the leg of what felt like corduroy, and then they had it out. Button's hands were numb. After they talked through how they would proceed, he held onto the case and partially opened a blade and then traced its V shape against the case to know which surface was which and then pried it against the turf until it opened. They had a knife!

Mabler went to work, dropped the blade and found it and began again and then most carefully with the edge of the blade flat against her wrist beneath the bond he turned the blade up and it freed her, and when she had some feeling back in her hands, she returned the favor by cutting away his bonds, and then forgetting their nakedness they blindly hugged before taking turns rubbing each other's wrists until circulation overpowered the needles.

"It's a man, and I guess he's dead. Here, help me roll him over; he's bound like we were. Now, we strip off his clothes. We'll split them among us." Button didn't want to strip a corpse and said so, but she got around it by focusing on her breathing. When they were done, he had a pair of boxer shorts and a T shirt beneath a too-short V-neck sweater, and she the corduroy pants cinched tight with a belt and what felt like a denim shirt, with wool socks on her feet. The boots wouldn't fit either of them, but they took the bootlaces and the knife and set out, edging around the outcrop and inching through the chink that funneled colder air, groping downward along the wall and into sable space.

~ ~ ~

Argon Kyrkcops gathered his disrobed flock in a circle ringed by smudge pots, and at the center and looming skyward stood a four-story rocket on a wide concrete pad. Scaffolding rose upward that supported a set of stairs that led to a high platform.

"Friends, the Winter Solstice is nigh upon us and hence we must embark on our emblematic trek, one that began with the arrival the Earth Mother, as predicted in the Cydonian Scrolls, and I say unto you her presence among the brethren and sistren continued to thwart the higher nature of mankind by promoting love of earth and not of the heavens. The scrolls tell us that the Native Americans and others were misled by the Earth Mother as a pawn of the bad Seven, recently divorced in echelon from the Pleiades and the evil twins of those with whom we seek communion, and that to do battle and defeat the Earth Mother they will send to us the anti-thesis of modern culture to do battle with her and thus uphold the scrolls' eschatology.

"The spaceships due to rendezvous with ours will carry away to heaven only those who have lengthwise and most strenuously sought a higher power: Atlanteans, Lemurians, Evangelicals of all Stripes, The Buffalo Brethren, Sisters of the Noogie Way, the Icarus Clan, Chanters de la Orthorhombic, Lustre of the Golden Mean, Ourobouros Union of the Milky Quartz, the Tantric Ormolu Pantheon, the Topaz Chicks from the point of their third CD, Tao Ntown, the Yin Minstrels of Qi, the Maidens of Moo, and the Mystic Knights of Moonstone Light for whom a lunar perigree will play a role in the realm of manifestation, for it is written that you can cast into and draw from the quartz your inmost intentions and the moonstone will bring to you the people or circumstances that will manifest reality, our reality, and that we can also cast into the stone to provide a shield against all that may come against thee without there being a wrinkle in the festivities, if you get my drift." He glanced up and down the rows.

They seemed to have gotten it as every ninth and nineteenth word had been a subliminal hypnotic key and they stood as one, swaying slightly and utterly numb to the frigid temperatures. He clicked on the recording of the remainder of the speech that would further set the scene and strode off stage to gather the players, well, all but one, for the final act and the syringes that would make them his opus' darling marionettes. After all, it had been predicted in his outline, had it not? Everything that he had written had come to pass and it had all been written here. When he'd first come to this place those many years ago, he had felt the presence of something unusual, grand, immeasurable under the yawning sky, as though that meadow was a focal point for the earth's magnetic field and then later on, he had sneaked back up by night and when he knew that Cody and company were elsewhere with their silly farming and markets or building that sorry excuse for a store. Every time he visited, he was rejuvenated, and he wrote like never before, doctrine for his bread and butter and stories to feed his passion, and the tales grew in richness and their depth and grandeur surprised and delighted him and the money and kudos began to roll in even though he had to keep it quiet and off the cuff; science fiction didn't mix well with fire and brimstone and besides, he had a new life and a family to lead it with. And then Cody built the dome and covered forever those chakras of the soil and his writing dried up and along with it the fervor that had kept him going for so long, and he could not handle a smoldering spleen; while he struggled with the loss of his true livelihood, what he utterly could not bear was his new reality strictly on its own merits, for while the church had been the ideal refuge, it was also a corral not meant to hold a stallion, a zebra, and a unicorn, and he was all of them, and more. It was then that he had re-opened the Revolution Box, one that had galvanized him like never before, a spur to action that outshined his former self and the lost literary glitter too, and ultimately led to this very moment.

He retrieved the clothing formerly belonging to his captives and headed to the sealed room. In a pocket of her jeans, he found an oval crystal and delighted at the thought of how he would force it into her mouth before he gagged it shut. The king would loom over her naked form in his trademark leathers and he would smite her as the spaceship's vapor trail lit the sky, and all would be right in the world. When he lowered the stairway that triggered the klieg lights and heat lamps and stepped down into the cavern, the recessed lighting cast an eerie green in an otherwise empty grotto and he controlled a scream. Empty? It was only then that he saw the naked man lying in the dirt with a gashed open head, his dear face a mass of caked blood. This time he did howl, and it sang through the cave like a siren.

~ ~ ~

"What in the hell was that?" cried Cody as he lunged up and around a boulder. They had all stopped behind Gertrude in the moment of the wail, for the bear stood up as though to gauge a sound wave pinging off the walls.

"Button told me of a singing or maybe chanting from somewhere in here," said Amanda.

"She was quite keen on it," said Ruth.

"We're on the right track then. She heard it; we heard it," stated Cody.

"Besides that, the bear has a bead on her," added Randal. As the flashlights traveled from face to face, Ruth alone remained quiet, but with head canted; she seemed to be listening.

"This mountain has a legend of chanting, one that goes back centuries, but I heard a different thing. Beneath that cry I thought I caught a man's voice and—wait! There it is." This time the lamps shifted to the front as the bear broke into a trot and with a cry of its own leapt into an antechamber that ran parallel to a lower but inaccessible passage; here two tunnels were alternately walled off where in the mountain's birth a river had once sluiced, gouging portals in the rock face of various dimensions but none larger than a small child, or a cub. Gertrude stuck her snout into one and the search party spelunkers fanned out and lined the little windows like tourists on a bus, when Millicent Tarbush hop-skipping from a ledge strode past clad only in Wellingtons and a sheer bodice and followed shortly after by a dancing shaft of light that became an even greater surprise when Jam Jeffries dropped down behind her and, spying the lamp beams lined up like ghostly fingers across the shaft, surmised the situation. "I don't know where she's headed, my friends, but I aim to keep her company like already through a mile of subterrane," and as his voice echoed off: "I'll besieging ya."

"Man," said Cody, "that old girl marched like one of those windup toys."

"Who is she?" said Randal.

"Why that was our—well, maybe I shouldn't say anything until we know more."

"Good thinking, Cody," said Ruth.

"Until now, I didn't know hypnotism was more than showroom histrionics," said Tarleton. He sipped from a hip flask, shined his light on it in offering, but had no takers.

"Well, I can tell you of what I have read at the library, my second home," said Ruth. "The entranced are actually in a state of intense focus and able to ignore everything going on around them, whatever the stimuli, which would go some ways toward explaining that nightdress, but the odd thing is that the experts who study it say that all hypnosis is self-induced."

Then, as though by signal, the bear started off and the train following after the ensorcelled and her escort up their parallel route, beams bouncing in the dark, but soon thereafter the twin chutes diverged, and they hiked on and upward, a ragtag cadre.

~ ~ ~

Up above in the daylight of afternoon another cadre was giving chase. Lou-Ann Strayhorn had reported to work and found no one in the reception area or in the office or, for that matter, in any of the rooms in the central building. She'd concluded that her chance to snoop around was finally at hand, given the secretive nature of the group, and it seemed a golden opportunity when she found eight steaming mugs of tea around a Ouija board, and in another room a legal pad with geometrical writing on it sitting beside a Jabba the Hut doll, and in still another a mound of Mylar (as though it had just fallen from the sky) in the center of a room lined with coffins on tiers. Investigating further she discovered the coffins were beds, as though every hour of sleep in one of them was a step in the final direction. Back in Argon's office she scoped the area behind his desk, and then on tiptoe entered his inner sanctum, a dark book lined den with a leather couch and a TV. On the coffee table sat dozens of neat stacks of - but in the gloom she couldn't be sure, and then a door behind her clicked and she raced off without looking and through the other door sidestepping Argon's desk as an arm raked her back and she raced down the hallway toward the front door with the footsteps pounding behind and all she thought of was the Mace and nightstick in her Jeep, but she didn't make it. The door swung open as she aimed her shoulder to ram it and she ran headlong into her boss knocking them both into the snow as the man chasing her had the gun knocked from his hand when Riggs swung a sap at his head and put his lights out. They handcuffed the baldheaded man and left him outside to prop open the door. Sheriff Bob Roberts adjusted his uniform and handed the loose pistol to Lou-Ann, and the three of them with weapons ready entered the compound of the Mystic Knights of Moonstone Light.

9

Button and her cohort Delray Mabler had kept to the wall and scooted along the sloping floor of their prison and then paused where the ceiling had shelved downward and it seemed obvious the two surfaces must meet and form a wedge, but they had felt a stronger breath now, puffs of colder air fanned their faces and they squirmed in its direction. Soon they had the ceiling at their backs.

"I can't go any more," cried Mabler.

"Don't stall now, Del, it's stronger here, can you feel it?"

"All I feel is my eyeballs about to get squeezed out."

She had listened to his gasping and assumed he was out of shape, but this was far worse. She wriggled back beside him.

"Del, it isn't much further and then we get out."

"You go on. I've had it."

"We can do it together, two's the magic number."

"I don't know."

"Think of what the King would do," she said, and nudged him with her head, all she could manage of a pat.

"The King wouldn't be in this shithole," he cried.

"Well, that is my point exactly, don't you see, we *are* getting out of here! You grab hold of my ankle and don't let go."

He moaned, but soon after she was towing him toward the assumed wedge end where murky indigo seeped toward them as they squirmed and little by little the floor angled more sharply downward but soon thereafter they had some headroom again and after squirming further were up and crawling on all fours in dusky light that turned to amber and the air in the passage, though brisk, had built to the strength of a breeze. They crawled and scooted and climbed and then left the dirt floor for one of ledges and jags of stone and every foot brought them into stronger light and cooler air, and then they stopped. Above them a crevasse rose like a chimney flue and they beheld a chalky sky through a spray of laurel.

Shivering now, they surveyed the crevasse: it went straight up for some twenty feet before angling off, and it took the wind out of her. Del caught the look in her abraded, grimy face and sprang to the defense; she had saved him from being buried alive, and he owed her.

"No glum looks now, young lady. You ever had a wedgie? Look at me, ever had a wedgie?" She shook her head. He thought: rescue those eyes!

"Well, it's when you get your underwear wedged in, you know?"

Her smile seemed to hold it in check, but she was misty.

"I'm about to show you the easiest way there is to get a wedgie," and he stepped into the crevasse and with his back to one side and his feet on the other, began to scrunch his way upward. She stood and watched him go up and pictured the wedgie and smiled once again.

"When I get up there, I will mark the spot and go—wait a second." With hands braced behind him he bounded off the wall and then was gone! But his head soon appeared, severed at the neck.

"There's a little ledge here running up about forty-five degrees. It's just about wide enough to lie down in sideways. It runs right up to the top: ready for your wedgie?"

Button considered the belt and bootlaces for a makeshift rope and gauged the distance, but in the end, she wedged her way to freedom and together they found the mountainside.

"Man, it's colder than Jack Frost's—"

"Jock itch. Dad says it every winter," she said, chattering teeth biting off the words. Huddled in a clump of frosted laurel, Button pointed. Before them was the compound and they joined hands and scampered from boulder to clump to tree until they had gained the pump house, the outermost shed, and in they went and grateful for its sheltering value, they hugged again. Then Button found a space heater under the work bench and cranked it, and they huddled over it stamping feet and clapping hands.

"Now what do we do?"

"We get warmed and, well—"

"Why isn't there a phone in here?!"

"This is just a—hang on just a second. Someone's coming." Through the small window they saw a man approaching bundled in a parka and toboggan.

"If he saw us, he wouldn't be taking his time."

"We've got to think fast," said Button. "I'll distract him, and you hit him."

On a shelf Mabler found empty oil cans and rags, a dusty light bulb, and a burlap potato sack. When he turned in despair, she was naked once again and posing languidly on the pump. He stepped behind the door as it creaked open and a young man entered, shut the door, and froze.

"Hey there sugar plum, how'd you like to warm me up?" The kid leered and took two steps forward before duty caught him short but Mabler dumped the burlap sack over his head, pinning his upper arms, and the three of them danced a desperate polka before they wrestled him to the floor where he thrashed about until Button drop-kicked him in the crown jewels, and he curled up and became still.

"Now it's my turn," she said, and stripped him from the waist down while Mabler straddled his back. Soon they had him hogtied to the pump stanchion and his mouth stuffed with rags. Button wrapped the belt around the head and cinched it, and they added on the warmest layers of their cast-off wardrobe which included the accessories of a flashlight, a multi-purpose tool and pouch, a tin of Redman filled, as she pointed out while chewing, caramel-coated cockroaches, a Zippo lighter, a half-pack of Camel straights and an item the size of a cell phone but without a display. They couldn't make it work. Mabler spat out the cockroach goo while Button put the thing in her pocket. She insisted that Mabler wear the boots, so they cut up the burlap bag and fashioned moccasins for her:

"Who says the Salvation Army never goes to war," she said, checking the window before they eased the door open and huddled in the lee of the shed as the wind picked up.

~ ~ ~

Argon Kyrkcops paced, following his shadow in circles beneath the towering dome while waiting for his team to arrive, but when they didn't show he hurried off toward the laundry room where a conversation was taking place.

"This is some joke? Where are Kip and Wylie?"

"Ain't seen 'em," said another.

"Sent Wylie to the office for—"

"I've just come from there. Kip has perimeter at this hour."

"It's not like him to be off somewhere, what you think Hal?"

"Something ain't right for sure, maybe we ought to fan out," said a fourth.

"Well, I got news for ya," said Hal, "Butch ain't around and the flock is on the launch pad, if he don't thaw them out quick, they're gonna freeze."

The gang started toward the assembly when their master appeared burdened with canvas satchels.

"The flock is okay," Butch said, reading their concern, "and to hell with the schedule, we're loading now, B.U.T.T. first. Got us a snake in the henhouse, boys. Get your guns."

They ran off and he cursed the rotten luck of losing *the seven*. They'd been together as a team and as loyal as gold for umpteen glorious years and never a hitch until Harvey bitched it and since then, things had slipped more counterclockwise; you could still tell the time, but it fucked your routine. S*even* was the key.

He had been taught that fact in the alien spacecraft and also in the seven whorls of the Pleiades and when he awoke at that Roy Rogers, or was that a different chapter, had followed a given path and wandered south, he recalled, to Atlantic City where every seven he rolled was a winner, and then playing with his instant wealth discovered to his great and lasting glee that when he narrowed his focus the sevens rolled over no matter what; why, it was a novel life. But casino crowds, he lamented, were peopled with unbearable automatons, and with his newfound power such company would have been a drain upon the intellect of a cockroach! Among the disenchanted there weren't numbers to count the losers, croupiers just rang the bell and Pavlov's monkeys jammed the turnstiles. Yet their very anonymity sparked ideas in him and put together story lines that often blurred into one another and melded identities.

Salvation came in the gradual layering of newly invented personas that he tried on, buttoned or zipped, and then cast off for the next garment line the way a gigolo dances between the beds of his lovers, and he kept one and wore it only when it gained him the best in flesh and fancy, in pets and power, and when flower power wilted he chose another road and that was how he had made his way here, and when you added it all up it was the sweet deal of the century and then Harvey, oh you sad, awful, stupid, sonofabitch. He snapped out of the past as Hal plus three arrived.

The smaller B.U.T.T. moved toward the stock-still flock, gathered from the ranked acres of willing to be anything Steppin Fetchits, his lovely mules, Butch thought, but then was stopped dead in his tracks as Mrs. Nungesser in a shear nightie loomed up out of the earth fifty feet away, offering carrots in her beseeching arms. Stupefied, he ran up to her.

"Madame," he intoned, but she marched on and he screwed his eyeballs into her psyche and droned again and she faltered in a downhill stutter step like an oscillating drunk but continued onward just as a man in a parka stumbled into sight. Hal let off a shot and the figure darted into the trees. Like a signal-gun, the shot seemed to set into motion the shuffling of the flock and with metronomic precision they emerged from the laundry laden with canvas sacks and headed for the rocket.

Riggs and company were moving in a step-by-step, room-by-room sweep of the main building as daylight waned and shadows armed with dusk crept closer. One large office held an executive-size desk and bookshelves lined with tidy rows of periodicals, an odd mixture of science fiction, mythology, and gardening. Riggs scanned copies of *Astronomy Argonaut, Mythos, Gemstones Today, Quark, Basal Basil* and others and then picked up a hefty pile of typed A-4 paper and attached to the cover page was a sticky note that read: "burn west from flashpoint – *Tumble!*" The Sheriff called him from down the hall, but he lingered a moment more, where had he heard that word, but then as he entered the dome's rotunda, they heard the shot, and as they ran from the room Jam sprinted past them down the hall and dove into an open coffin-bed and whisked the lid shut. After a minute he lifted it and perceived rapid gunfire and said aloud:

"Man, guns are way uncool! Phallic props for the penis invidious! Disjointed dickheads ready to fuck up whatever world they encounter!" he cried aloud but then he thought of Button and came alert and rolled out of the crypt, streaked back down the hall but came to a stop beneath the dome and stood for a moment and latched the distance there, the beauty in it, the peaceful vibes, and then walked directly to the niche, slid a panel aside and stepped down onto the catwalk of the timber frame between the foundation and the earth, their earth, before dropping onto it and locating the chute, memory nudged by the odd finger of light, and squeezed himself down its length and dropped into the cavern. When he and Cody and their pals had excavated the root cellar, digging it all by hand, the installation of lights was vetoed in favor of its natural, earthen spirit as well as that of it being off the grid as much as was doable, but then it only got a couple season's use anyway. But he remembered Button hiding in here when the whole mountain went ape shit looking for her and that rabbit. Or was it the other cellar, this one's twin, over on the south side where they'd stored their bushels of homegrown? Well, they both met somewhere here, and he'd check 'em out. A moan so startled him he turned and whacked his funny bone on a pull-down set of stairs that he'd been standing beside yet hadn't noticed, then groping about found prone beneath a fissured crag that had been their air vent refrigeration system, a naked Jensen Tarbush, struggling to rise. He carried the boy up the stairs and into the dome and laid him down. The nearest water he knew of was snow and he dashed outside into the pandemonium that swirled beyond the walls with shouts and shots and shadows and scooped a hatful and ducked back in and kneeling beside the injured boy got him clean enough to see a nasty wound that needed attention, but what to do? Button . . . he could sense her presence or was it twenty years of her in everything about this place, a spark that leaped and arced between everyone she engaged such that it was hard to separate what he wanted in that moment from what he knew, the one clouding the smiling sun of the other, and here of all places was like not going to work, man. Okay, find a phone and—people coming—find out what in hell is going on, and he nearly leaped as Button entered the room with Mabler close behind, a pair of scarecrows. They threw a rug over Jenson and then through the hugging and jabbering they worked out what they thought was going on, and then Mabler led them to Argon's office and they called for an ambulance. There was no answer at the Sheriff's office. Mabler volunteered to stay with the kid when a Deputy entered the room, got the situation sized up for her, and set to work on the boy. That was cool with Jam, and Button too was relieved, feeling sad for Jensen in a manner she couldn't express except to say that she'd had enough surprises for one day, a remark she'd later remember as trite.

In the rotunda they bypassed the alcove stairs and by using the wainscoting rail as a step, Jam boosted Button up and then a further step onto his shoulders gained her the rim-walk tread that ran the circumference of the interior of the dome (one that allowed for its cleaning with a long-handled brush, or for reading the constellation charts that had once been posted beneath the lower edge of the glass). Jam then boosted Mabler up in the same manner and then he clambered up after and together they took in the view: downhill and off to the right two lines of naked people worked back and forth between the laundry building and the rocket ship like worker ants, hauling satchels and boxes and bags, amidst a gun fight in progress between the sheriff and the bald headed kidnappers, yet the shooters from both sides held their fire every time a cult member came stick-walking, to and fro, but breaking free of the baggage chain and angling off momentarily only to come stumble-stepping back into line and the combatants between them weren't getting much shooting done, and in one of these lapses Button saw him beside the rocket hatchway flagging his arms in a manic semaphore at a fat lady she recognized as Mabler's chanteuse and, great heavens, can it be?

"I'm going down there."

"No way Button, the guns—"

"He's not getting away with this!"

"Let the Sheriff handle it. He'll have called for backup by now," said Jam.

"Ms. Springfield," said Mabler, grabbing her wrist, "in my time here I noted when they were naked, they were catatonic, went about like sleepwalkers, but when dressed they had their own willpower. Thing is, it's that silvery stuff; whatever controls them can't penetrate it. Remember how he moved us around like chess pieces?"

Jam couldn't get the objection out of his mouth before Button and Mabler had clambered down and squirmed into the one-piece Mylar suits and grabbed up as much as they could carry. Jam joined them. "Well, if I can't talk you out of it, I'm coming with you," he said, and dressed accordingly.

Stepping from the dome they encountered a pair of rusting cultists, blue with cold. Working the shivering duo into the Mylar and then into the dome, that act was repeated as they made their way across the hill and clothed the naked as they went, but they were going to have to traverse the gunfight to get to the rocket. At the belch of a throaty scream, Button stepped from behind a tree to witness one of the chrome dome cretins who had assaulted her bolt from a woodpile with a charging bear at his heels and followed by her, Cody and Amanda, and Ruth and Randal and the entire farmer's market crowd and she leapt and shouted a measure of it, for what a spectacle it was! By then two chrome domes were on the ground and the others had their hands in the air amid the naked and clothed all in a swirl and then she lost sight of all that and sprinted through the melee and scooted downhill with Mabler at her heels and a great shouting all around and Gertrude growling and distant sirens wailing up the switchbacks.

~ ~ ~

With escape thwarted before his eyes, in one mighty effort Kyrkcops ramped his egress Qi to eject those vibes that had cemented Mrs. Nungesser in the hatchway, but he quavered and couldn't zero in, there being too much interference on the diode, too many chakra misfires, and too damned many of his mules getting their silicon back! Unable to budge her from half in and half out, he cursed his own prediction of this event; could he have scripted this? Throwing the carrots into the snow he bounded up the scaffold stairs two at a time unaware of pursuit and entered the rocket through the top hatchway and secured it as his erstwhile Earth maiden and Righteous king ascended the last flight of stairs, not acting their script either. Moments later a thunderclap stilled the action on the hill and a ball of fire roiled from the launch pad and the rocket began to rumble and shake with a fury that ejected Mrs. Nungesser who, upon lumbering to her feet, passed out as Millicent Tarbush and in the arms of Riley County deputy Lou-Ann Strayhorn who wrapped her in a parka. Button and Mabler raced back down the scaffold stairs and sprinted into belching smoke of the rocket engine banging and booming and onward into the hatchway they bounded and began climbing a ladder up through the ship as it caterwauled and the metal surfaces shivered and rivets popped and then a great roaring broke and they threw themselves to the deck and hugged in fear and then the floor became the wall.

Randal and Tarleton and the search party team and their prisoners and everyone else out on the hill stood still and gazed upward, speechless to help or prevent such boldness when Button and another chased a baldheaded man wrapped in tinfoil up the stairs all the way to the nosecone only to race back down again and run through fire and enter the rocket ship that, moments later, roared fifty feet off the launch pad until it met the treetops when it teetered, and toppled like a tree from a logger's saw. When it slammed into the ground the impact bounced it lengthwise back into the air, one end the near apex of its flight, before it rolled downhill like a spindle until it hit stumps amidships and spun on its axis as the nosecone blew off and a glowing metal chunk flew high into the evening sky, then hurtling toward, a space heater landed with the clang of sprung parts, and the wintry snow silence again descended and no one moved for what seemed to Randal the longest moment of his life, before they all bolted like racers.

Smoke poured from rivet holes and between the seams and from other cracks in the broken frame as the rocket hissed and rattled and the air was filled with a stench that watered the eyes. First into a popped-open hatchway was Cody with Randal behind him as Amanda elbowed him aside and went in behind her husband. The three of them crawled over small mountains of canvas sacks, some of the contents loosed upon the deck in a shifting cereal of freeze-dried larvae and greenbacks, calling out for their beloved.

Meanwhile, Harlan Riggs had sprinted downhill, twice losing his footing and eating snow, and approached the part of the ship where it had been ripped open like a tin can, with gun drawn he shouted, freeze this is the FBI, but his voice cracked, and the pronouncement came out sounding like a duck. Then poised at the edge of the hatchway, pistol at his ear, he estimated, he determined, he formulated: what he was hearing was laughter and he poked his nose around the frame.

"Get off ma leg Del! Yah ha ha!"

"Ca-ca-can't! It's down hee down, tee hee, your pants! Hoo ooh hoo!"

"Something damn sure is, ahahhaha this is what a middle leg feels like!"

"Move your butt!"

Riggs ducked into the crumpled, cockeyed cockpit and beheld an upside-down Ms. Springfield and Elvis Presley, their limbs interwoven through twisted stowage, giggling like children.

"Where is he?"

They howled louder.

"I said, where is he! The man who calls himself Argon?" He spun suddenly at a noise behind him and whacked his head on a broken beam and went to his knees as Gertrude poked her nose in his face and licked the blood.

"Oh god! A bear!" yelped Del, and it set Button off again and she laughed her security to its resolve.

"Why, Gertrude honey, is that you?" The bear had nudged a breathless Riggs aside and canting her head, beheld her friend and licked her face which sent Button again down corridors of laughing until the bear began rooting from spilled sacks of bug meal and then bloody Riggs was there beside them as shouts for Button could be heard elsewhere in the rocket.

Before long as many as could fit into the mangled cockpit were jammed together and everyone yelling and pulling on the metal that pinned the girl and the crooner, but they didn't succeed until Ruth coaxed her giant pet away from the bug banquet and harnessed her to one end of a come-along rustled up by Jam, and the pair tumbled free. Hugs and backslaps and high fives all around were brought up short as a collective realization dawned: someone who should have been among them was missing, and they filed out to count heads. Outside of the hissing, smoking rocket, mixed with the snow and scattered greenbacks, they stood ankle deep in a vile, putrescent goo that smelled like rotten vegetation, a summer smell, and there came along with it, as though the proverbial light bulb had clicked on in concert: where was that guy, known to some as Argon and to one of them as a different man entirely, and each recounted their version of his race up the stairs and into the cockpit before the rocket began its ascent or descent, depending on who you talked to, and once again they were jabbering and gesticulating, each conducting a madcap orchestra, all that is, except Jam.

"The nosecone is gone, looks like a big green bubble set in a silver band."

"How would you know that, mister?" said Riggs.

"Shoot, I sold it to 'em."

"You are under arrest as a material—"

"You will not arrest him!" cried Button, setting herself between the two of them as she covered her nose and mouth against the stench.

"You'll have to arrest me too."

"And me!"

"Us too!" The smell was truly awful, but the agent had his back to a bear as the goo stung and watered his eyes. He waved them off before covering his mouth.

"Only thing makes sense," said Cody behind a scarf, "that nosecone must've cartwheeled. My guess is it's hung up in a tree somewhere down there."

The snow-covered hills were steep and dark and cold. Again, the town group formed as two search teams and went down the slope, city boys bringing up the rear, but the women who had re-entered the rocket were having a pow-wow. Button waved off Randal's attempt to join them, and when he asked her how best to traverse a winter slope, she turned her back on him. Perplexed, he hustled off, slipping and skidding on snow slicked by rocket ooze, to catch up to Tarleton who was struggling to follow the zigzag pattern of descent set by Cody and Jam. Soon, back in clean air, they were both sliding on their butts as they grabbed hold of branches and staubs to slow their pace, but several times went careening into others, knocking them off their feet amid a flurry of curses at the city boys in their city shoes what couldn't handle snow. By the light of the rising moon, they had yet to see anything but trees and were wondering how long the hill ran and whether that thing could have bounded over the creek and landed God knows where.

Randal recalled stories he'd read of the wild but which now featured the tangent of a giant bouncing ball crossing the slopes of the Appalachians but headed for the stars and with a man inside strapped to a chair, goggles, white scarf trailing. The group came to a halt at a level space on a high bank, trail end of a ledge where a stream cut the ridges in two, and below, moonlight glinted on the rippled water and lit the creek bed enough to see that something down there floated in a pool, something unlike its surroundings, for boulders had no sheen to them nor did they loll from side to side and glisten like smoky quartz. Fixated, they gaped as one at a crystal ball that bobbed like a Brobdingnagian tea cup in Brindle Creek.

It was decided that Cody, Jam, the Sheriff, and Riggs would go down and inspect the nosecone and remove its occupant from the stream. Cody allowed as how they would find a rag doll. The others headed across the slope to round up the other search party and left Randal and Tarleton to climb the hill on their own.

Thirty minutes later they came huffing within sight of Button who stood beside her mom and Ruth down slope and at an angle to where the crumpled rocket lay as they watched Gertrude pawing the earth and tossing tufts behind her. Tarleton flopped down, blowing hard, and Randal struggled on over to join Button, hugs on his mind, frozen feet forgotten and soon he was beside her, but she ignored him. Amanda told him about a feature of the land up here, their land, in the context of what Gertrude had apparently found. The ridges were speckled with air vents and caves some little bigger than a human hand. One of them cored through the mountain and emerged just south of where she and Cody had built the dome, and she now traced her memory, and Ruth too had that faraway look. Then, as Gertrude roared, they knew that she had gained access. Amanda knew where this tunnel led and came to two conclusions: the men were on a goose chase and Argon (Not argon! stated Button) had given them the slip.

Following a huddle of all concerned, Amanda, down on all fours, followed Ruth who trailed Gertrude into the cave and were in turn followed by Button and Randal and lastly by a revived Tarleton who confessed his shivering was due to being soaked under his coat. Ruth said he'd be fine and the cave would be warmer still but to keep the coat on. Soon they were headed up, flashlight beams dancing, while Button endured Randal's questions before finally swinging around to face him.

"You should have been there for me! Where were you?"

"Sweet, c'mon I was in jail."

"You were drunk! If you'd been sober, they wouldn't have done what they did!"

"Babe, c'mon, you're not being reasonable."

"I am not your *babe* and—"

"Is everything okay back there?" called Amanda. Button marched on and left Randal dumbfounded, with Tarelton consoling.

Before long the party came to a head-high earthen wall and Amanda explained they would have to boost each other up to gain the next cavern, and that it opened on a chute that led diagonally up, either into an adjacent cavern or to the dome on top of the hill; she wasn't sure.

"You got us all in here, you don't know where it goes," said Randal.

"Don't snarl at her, son, she knows more than you. And Gert and I will wait right here in case he tries coming back this way," said Ruth.

"I have long admired your spirit, Ruth dear," said Amanda, "but there's nothing back there, you think about it; our man is headed up, and so should we all; we need Gertrude. And hey, Randal, you work out the yah yahs, you hear? And just so you know, these tunnels have been here for thousands of years, and it would take about that long to map all of 'em. Besides, there's only two we know on this side of the ridge, and they both lead to the dome, isn't that right, hon?"

"Right as a rain dance," said Button as she and the other two women and the two men boosted Gertrude up over the wall, and then each other.

10

Argon Kyrkcops was having a difficult time shuffling about and dragging what he feared was a broken leg while cradling a useless arm that he'd wrapped with an ace bandage and then slung around his neck the loose end and cinched a knot with his teeth. Still, he had been able to gather a dozen sacks of cash into a backpack along with two passports. He stuck the Glock in his belt, but what he wanted the most was up there, and again he looked up through the dome toward the heavens and sighted the rim-walk in the shadows and began to edge toward the alcove stairs one belabored inch at a time, sweating worse now but he was doing it, and had found where planting the foot brought the least pain. The alcove opened at his touch and he collapsed against the inside wall, sliding the panel shut behind him and steadied his breathing and measured it: ten minutes to get up the steps and that back down, maybe less. He started up and shooting stars danced in his eyes and he imagined them falling far down the ridge in the woods below.

"Did you see that?" Delray Mabler had his head back and arm out even though he himself was but a walking shadow at the end of the combined search parties headed back up the ridge and following a fuming Jack Riggs and by Cody who pondered the mysteries of the mountain and the glory of a night sky, like a million pin prick holes in an ancient black umbrella, said Jam. Soon they came within sight of the rocket and wondered again how anyone inside that nosecone could have survived. The best guess was that his body flew out of the vehicle and was broken up somewhere out there, and that tomorrow they would have to retrieve it before wildlife did, or they'd never find it.

Away from the rancid guacamole of the hissing rocket, the hill was mostly quiet but littered with Mylar and spilled money sacks and windblown bills and the catch-all you-name-it random detritus of pandemonium as the devoted and formerly so had scrambled for cover or release; most were found huddling in sheds or wandering the compound and were being brought along, herded by deputies, while beneath them all a bear and her friends had also found release.

After they had crossed the cavern, they ogled an earthen slide that angled upward toward dim light. Before anyone could speak, Button crawled in and they could hear her scrabbling away. There came a short whistle and they went up the chute in single file just as gingerly as they could and fanned out at the apex to await Gertrude who, while she had claws to drag herself forward, was about as wide as the trough. While they waited, Button wandered into the shadows to discover Jam's old fruit crates stacked along a wall. In them were tidy piles of rubber-banded paper several inches thick. She called her mother over and they huddled until they heard the bear's approach. Gertrude shoved her paws out of the chute, laid her head on them, and went to sleep.

Overhead loomed the joists of the pentagonal ten by ten foundation frame of the dome. Between two of them they found the pull-down stairs that Jam had taken note of earlier, and it struck Amanda with that out of whack appeal of incongruous images, like a pair of sneakers looped over a telephone wire, yet one more of so many things that seemed out of place from long ago, like with razor wire and security cameras. Back then, it had been easy to hop down several feet to the earth floor or hoist themselves up onto the frame. Now, on the mother and daughter wavelength, they both saw not a stair but a gateway for a bear. Ruth shook her head and allowed as how the dear had already had a very long day, hiking and caving and whatnot. Amanda pulled, the stairs unfolded, and they urged the great beast to wake up, but Gertrude's reply was a snore, so they climbed up in single file, Button in the lead, and split up to search the different rooms.

Riggs and party had reached the rocket and sat in the muck for a breather, the stench having dissipated. Cody went around picking up greenbacks as the agent reminded him not to stuff his pockets; it was evidence and would be treated as such. Too bad, said Cody, we could use it to start us a fire, keep warm out here until everyone is accounted for. Well, we could use the rocket, somebody said. No, spoke another, it could flash up at any minute; it is still burning down inside.

Riggs had a moment. "Say that again."

"What, the rocket, well, we can't go in there!"

"No, what did you say, *flash,* yeah, that's it! It was *flashpoint*!" That word on Argon's desk also triggered two memories that had teased him for months and they both featured the Reverend, first there was the deer hunt, and then at the protest—he had said: *brisance.* A man of the cloth wouldn't use those terms, but a bomber sure as hell would. And this rocket, he sniffed the air, is a colossal garbage bomb! Riggs motioned to the Sheriff and they hiked as fast as they could go up the ridge. Sensing that something was up, Mabler, Jam, and Cody followed after Riggs who was headed for the dome while others began scooping up money and pondering where to hide it.

From their search of the buildings, Riggs and the Sheriff knew the only access to the polygon or whatever the thing was called was from the main hallway, and so they headed further up to the parking area and the front entrance. Lagging behind, Mabler followed Cody and Jam to a downslope section of the structure's stone base before Cody hoisted himself up and was followed by Jam who helped him pivot a metal grating and the two helped Mabler scramble up and traverse the slot from which they accessed the dome through a panel in the alcove wall as Jam reflected on their youthful fondness for secret passageways to nooks for hiding contraband weed.

~ ~ ~

Inside the giant eye all was hushed except for the whisper of furnace air through floor ducts, and now washed by the red and blue emergency lights that pulsed like heartbeats. Button knew the dome was silent for a reason, and it was no reason that any other could fathom, for she had breathed life into this space in every day that she lived in its spell, and she knew even when she had grown old enough to play outside that when she left the dome behind it had ceased to breathe, and then lay dormant for years, only to become a habitat for personalities layered in such deceit as to likely shut it up forever, but prayed that wasn't so. She motioned *no talking* and moved along the wall toward the Taurus niche, gliding silently, and Amanda followed behind, stepping exactly where her daughter had, and noting the pantomime, Randal did likewise. Soon Button had gained the niche and something different caught her ear, and at first, she believed the dome had come awake to her presence, but the sound was a whimper; someone softly crying. She eased in a little further and paused: the sound was coming from above, where she and Mr. Jiggs had their play space overlooking the room where séances spoke the names of the heavens and peopled them with heroes. She went up.

Leaning against the glass and holding a satchel stuffed with papers, Button confronted the man she had chased to the rocket, but he looked different as he shuffled toward her, smiling.

"I'm glad you are here. Help Q to the stairway; I have injured myself."

He came closer and, in the half-light, she saw it was not that man. Had she seen him before? She wasn't sure, but he was hurt, and as she reached to assist him felt herself go dreamy, and then by helping each other, together they made it down the stairs to the anteroom where a brisk cross draft sent loose papers fluttering from the satchel. Button bent to retrieve them and when she handed them up, it was to the Reverend Tarbush.

"You've come just in time, my dear. I took a frightful tumble racing up here to help. I got the call on my CB. Good thing Bob Roberts made me a deputy, yes indeed, a good thing. And of course, I have had the RFD badge for twenty years. I was just worried sick, and then when I heard you'd been found, well we all drive a little too fast, don't we?" He took a step backwards and winced. Then he took another.

She couldn't recall how she had come to be there and the ensuing confusion stumbled her thinking, but now wait a second, what about Gertrude? The thought seemed absurd, and yet familiar, like a fragment of a dream recalled at midday. She looked at him again and then at the papers clutched in her hand and a focus returned to her, and he caught the light in her eyes.

"By the way, I want out of our little one act plays, our theatre as we call it."

She felt herself coming unstuck as from a gooey mass - something clicked and she popped into place, saw him again, but only as she ever had.

"I never called it that, you did," she said, "and it doesn't matter anyway. You were in it to work through your kinks, massage them or pump them up. But I was just doing it for the money."

"Were you?" He edged further away. "No, that is only your flaccid excuse for an utter lack of morals; following the primrose path of your sleazy parents who took away a priceless meadow and ruined it for all time!"

"What are you going on about, and morals? You're one to talk. You've got all the morals of a gutter spout. What's worse, you spread that drainage all over the county. People listen! They take your words as truth!"

He bent and picked up a backpack and with some trouble, slung it on.

"You're not even their spry, look at you! A primrose path lined with beds, but not flower beds. You don't even know who your parents were." She hissed at him but also felt a quiver of yield. She didn't look like Amanda and Cody, or anyone in the commune, but knew that when your personal springtime bloomed, pistil yearned for stamen, or other pistil, or variations as wild as the wind, and that was perfectly okay.

"Give me those."

"What do we have here," she said, "a clipping from a Roanoke paper, 'robbers hit the Surety Bank and Trust in Glenwillow shopping center' and another, hmmm, the Charlotte Observer: 'Bank robbed in daring daylight raid.' Now Rev, whatever would you want with—" and the night in Randal's kitchen flashed a signal that jolted other more recent memories and slotted them into place like an index, and catching the look on her face he was beside her then with a gun in his good hand.

"Keep your pretty little mouth shut. We're going outside and drive away from here, just the two of us."

She felt the gun pressed against her, but her resolve fought back.

"You going to kill everyone the way you did poor Jensen?"

"No! No! I didn't hurt him; it was - wasn't me."

They had reached the alcove and Button lunged with her hip and Tarbush whacked his arm on the jamb and shrieked as she ducked out of the panel and rolled away and without another thought sprinted from the anteroom and around the curving wall and gained the central area where she screamed, he's over there, over there at Taurus! He's got a gun! In an instant she had Amanda and Randal and Tarleton and Ruth for backup, and at the sound of her yelling her dad and Jam and Mabler too, and they all turned as one as a man in a parka and carrying two backpacks shuffled from the anteroom, wheezing and dragging a leg, and Button was dumbstruck that not one of the gathered appeared to recognize him.

"He's back in there," the man said. "He fell down, maybe wounded." They raced away across the great room, all but Mabler and Randal who remained at

Button's side. There was shouting behind them and commotion out front. Smiling, the man spread his arms.

"Friends, if I may ask a favor?" Button was ready.

"He is not who he pretends to be."

"Who does he pretend to be?" said Randal, and Mabler pointed a knowing finger when a voice behind them said:

"Ralph Bannister, that's who."

"No, he is Doctor Argon Kyrkcops, a fake southerner, and a mean one at that!" said Mabler in reply to Harlan Riggs who now stood beside him. Amanda, Cody, and Jam re-entered the room and stood to the side, adjacent to where the Sheriff stood, ogling the ceiling, and Cody reflected that this was the only time the old boy had gotten this far inside without a warrant. Amanda thought the Reverend looked out of sorts, and then thought they all would after a night like this.

Reverend Tarbush looked at her and spoke:

"It is a night such as this that reminds us all of our duty to be guided beside the still waters and comforted in the vale of our weaknesses before the—"

"Don't listen to him," shouted Mabler, "he's got those things in there, what do you call 'em, make you do things!" Mabler plugged his ears and Button followed suit, and Randal too but not before he caught the rising brimstone.

"—wherein the valediction of the mighty cast aside the barriers of the halt and forlorn and yea cast aside also the gates of wrath that there be egress of the sure and august," and he moved forward then to part them with locution and got as far as Button who drew back and clocked him a good one, and he staggered and swiveled then to face alternately one group and then the other and in his whirling they appraised a change in him like the shift of a mimic's guise, and when he stood back once again his eyes blazed like crystals.

"The Mighty Argon commands you to kneel!" he droned as his eyes went wide and he willed them obey. Jam knocked into Cody, but both kept their feet and Amanda felt a hand caress her and the Sheriff danced with ants in his pants and all were distracted until Riggs strode up and grabbed Argon's wrist only to be flung aside like a papier-mâché doll that impacted with a wall and struggled to arise. Argon made for the hallway as Button howled:

"Stop! You are not walking out of here you son of a bitch!"

Behind the partition that shielded the anteroom there came a growl and Gertrude charged into the room and down the hall, bowling over a frozen Argon who had turned to cackle at an outraged earth mother and a righteously pissed off king, foils to an end predicted somewhere in the scrolls of his own imagination.

When they urged Gertrude aside, the man in the parka was raving and drooling and prattling on in languages nobody understood. Riggs read him his rights anyway and handcuffed him. Sheriff Bob Roberts led his old friend away, hardly recognizable now except to one who did seem to know him, for she stepped up and kissed him.

"Augie, what has happened!? Where are we? Why are we here? Augie!?" A dazed Millicent Tarbush stood conflicted and alone until she too was led down the hallway by a nurse, and followed soon thereafter by the Springfield family, arm in arm. Randal stood with Mabler and Tarleton like old buddies, but none of them spoke as Ruth gathered Gertrude the Bear and said, keep in touch.

~ ~ ~

In the new semester Button returned to classes determined to have her best year yet, having been reinvigorated daily by the company of her family and friends in and among Rainbow Run, Blue Jay Way, and the revived Round Wilson Celestial Center, as well as by all of the town folk who had joined the search parties, faces she had known but rarely spoken to, stopping in to wish her well or inquire after her health. She took a special interest in helping to rip out the galvanized posts, chain-link fencing, and the after-market (looks like the real thing!) plastic razor wire that once again opened the land to the people.

A once-again healthy Jensen Tarbush also returned to school but struggled to focus and often kept to himself until Button opened him up like a blossom one wintry day with one of those smiles that will launch a sundog on a cloudless day. She did it again the next day and then often enough that they got to talking again and patched up their differences. He dismantled PETPEv after a well-known chemical pesticide company had threatened a lawsuit following another botched protest, and he decided to focus his green energies and evolving world view on the Kudzu problem, and formed a new campus group called Southern Gothic, for the weed is truly a haunting, is it not? They hung out together, but he demurred in tagging along when she was subpoenaed to answer some questions and then finalize the statement she had made to the FBI.

She joined her family on the courthouse steps in Ashville and in they went together, each separately reliving the tragic events of a Christmas better forgotten, yet tattooed. She answered the questions put to her and tried hard not to make eye contact with Agent Riggs. After reading her statement she thought about Jensen and his shattered family, and said:

"This last part here, I am not sure who I saw."

"Miss," said a woman in a navy-blue suit, "don't allow him wiggle room."

"Aw heck, Darcy, it won't matter. Just where would he go, anyway?" said Riggs.

"He'd go home," said Button.

"Not to that kind of home he wouldn't. Let me tell you something. For twenty some years that man lived a double life, and when he got bored with the mundane tasks that we all do, he started robbing banks under another pseudonym and lived that life for another twenty years until he split off again as a cult leader; now he's got four layers and I tell you, all that duplicity took its toll; he's so far around the bend he's come full circle." Button signed the paper, and then picking up her bag and coat, she paused:

"I would like to see him."

"Out of the question."

"No, it is imperative that I see him just this once, for one moment."

"And what is your reason?"

"I need to know, to see, to visualize that man and his cage. I need to know it in my heart that he is truly there and will be there, and what that box looks like. I'm not afraid of him, and I never was, but I fear what he is capable of doing. I won't leave until you show me." Riggs regarded her a moment and then huddled with his colleagues.

"You'll be happy to know that he will soon be moved to an institution for the criminally insane where he will languish for the rest of his days," said Riggs, as they entered a darkened room, one she recognized as alike Randal's description. Behind the two-way mirror sat Jensen's father, but when the agent switched on the sound, she listened to a casting call:

". . . and when death knocks on your door and hands you your walkin' shoes, you will not be lifted up by the chariots of Chevrolet; you will not be lifted up by the chariots of Oldsmobile; you will not be lifted up by the chariots of Cadillac. No, brother, if you have not worshipped every good day of your life, if you have not kept the crease in the pants of your faith, if you have not punished

your children severely for stealing from the cookie jar, then brother you will ride a chariot of fire without air bags and you will ride a chariot of fire without cruise control and you will ride that chariot of fire, brother, down to Red's Barbeque of eternal damnation across the street from the Junkyard of Souls!

"No, it ain't a sole plan it is our plan so don't gimme that weasel funk, Harvey, this job is easy pickin'. Okay, let's go over it one more time. Driver: Harvey; Shotgun: Kip; Organic Mechanics: Wylie and Hoke; Runners: Hal and Flip. As always, I am the inside man and they will freeze, the ones resist get greased a double dose; Mechanics join me over the counters for the grab; then we vamoose as I freeze 'em once more from the door ... for it is written in the Cydonian Scrolls that the uroboros is the serpent of light that shines within me as ... I ply the lenticular fields of the stellar gravisphere on the booster rocket approach to Nibiru in the shadow of Aquarius ...."

Button turned from the window and strode from the room and hurried off down the corridor. Riggs caught up to her on the sidewalk where she hugged her parents.

"Cody Springfield, I owe you an apology." Agent Harlan Riggs chewed on a toothpick and waited as Amanda waited and Button also held her breath. No one said a thing, so the agent, now known to everyone in the valley to have been a liar, got in his truck and drove away. They stood on the corner, arms linked, and soon smiled at the approach of the familiar van, and piled inside to head home.

"You get it all done?" said Jam.

"There is still the nasty bit of testifying, if it gets to that," said Cody, looking out the back window at the courthouse and its silly monument to some man whose money lent his name to the construction of justice, and he thought of its drab interior, what Riggs must be like inside.

"Dad, why didn't you accept his apology and just be done with it?"

"He had everybody stereotyped from the get-go. I wasn't about to justify it, much less a conversation with him. He's gone and let us hope it's for good." Button ruminated on that and then also on others that had departed, Randal among them. There was Mrs. Tarbush who had gone away, and folks said it was Lou-Ann Strayhorn went with her, not that it mattered a hoot, and Delray Mabler and his family had also vanished one night without so much as a farewell, but then she figured he had too much to gain back if he were to lose it all again. The entirety of the cult had drifted away as though they had come from vapor and only materialized as their leader had penned them into existence, and the compound too stood empty, but she believed it was refilling itself with golden silences and whispers, and figured it would not be haunted by the little sleight of hand that her dad said was none of their doing: the money stolen by B.U.T.T and that accumulated in the rocket far exceeded what had been reported taken in the robberies, at which point Cody had sealed the cavern beneath the dome to await further developments, and there had been none; Jam's old fruit crates became Button's college fund.

But she felt it was Randal's going that she missed the most, and she hoped that he would come to an understanding of why she had been unable to forgive him. After all, he did try to make it up: his bravery on the hill that night spoke legions about his character that she both admired and swooned over, but the chink in her aura had been heartfelt; it pierced deep down where love's unmeasured well resides, and to a depth she only sensed at, but a tangible depth and one to be plumbed only with a lover whose own depth would measure hers stride for stride, always there, always certain; but Randal's absence the day of her abduction didn't fit the profile regardless of his charms, and she wasn't going to have that yawning chasm between them, stuck there forever. She needed it removed and she sensed that in time she would indeed find it gone and so be able to love him once again, just as she knew that by then he would be but a memorable shadow. As Jam headed them home, she blew him a kiss out the back window and watched the distance recede, Randal within it, to what would never again be the same.

In the initial aftermath of Button's departure from his life, Randal was too stunned by events to be much more than an observer on the outside, looking in. But then a yawning hollowness took place at his core and it was there he came to understand that the path his life had been merrily skipping along had ended abruptly in thickets, and their brambles held him in stasis; while he plod about his business—attending classes and writing for the paper—he sensed the scansion of Time and events go by at a measured, metronomic pace like he never had, and sensed too that love's meter is all its own, that romance players get swept along through acts and scenes with little regard for the middling, plebian chores of day to day; it is for lovers alone that their worlds, spinning within the larger orbit, are cycled in rosy light from dawn to dusk, aglow in moonlight. When spun from the axis by Fortunes wheel and into an elliptical wobble, only shards of that light remained, felt more than seen, for glinting slivers would never fill that core but rather wistfully scrape at it, carving the hollow deeper. On the occasions when the two ran across each other on campus, Randal couldn't bear the moment, and scurried away. More and more he also fled the newsroom and its happy-go-lucky batch of hacks and hounds as Tarleton would teasingly call them, and it didn't go unnoticed. Over the protestations of his friend and mentor, he was fired, but he took it and rolled with the punch; another descent just then was unthinkable, and so he declared a double major and buried himself within his studies in journalism/communications and linguistics, the former to obtain the credential he had otherwise lacked, and the latter, well, he'd been drawn to language (as a field) for some time without any conscious knowledge of it: from his parents' habitual yelling to the various drawls of characters befriended, from Elmer Butkins to Mr. Cobb to Merle Terrell, to Jam and Amanda and Cody's adopted Southern-ese with its Brooklyn overlay, the spoken language so different by region and locale, and that particularly true of the Hydra headed Argon Kyrkcops / August Tarbush / Ralph/-Butch Bannister, not to mention the French inflections of his long-suffering wife Millicent / Mrs. Nungesser, each personality tooled with its own dialect and lexicon to match, raving lunatic or eloquent orator, take your pick, and then there was his (Argon's too) penchant for writing and its relationship to the spoken word that begged the question, which was primary and which derivative?

While he was yet too busy to be aware of it, Randal's life was soon skipping along a divergent path, one that found his background knowledge, writing, and communication skills to be of great use as he barreled onward to graduate theses, but more importantly he reemerged whole again, surely wounded (Hey Cupid, aim that thing elsewhere!) and wary, but full again, armed now with the surety of a new life, and that adventure was lurking somewhere, awaiting him.

The End

About the Author

After graduating high school, other than a brief stint at Naropa Institute to study poetry with luminaries of the Age, Steven Mooney was for twenty years an unskilled blue-collar laborer working as a custodian, garbageman, groundskeeper, librarian, messenger, seasonal firefighter, taxi/truck driver and earning just enough money for the books he devoured across the breadth of English and American literature. Tiring of the shanty life at thirty-eight, he ventured to college and earned a Bachelor of Art in English and a Master's in Education where he first encountered ESL. For the next twenty years he taught English in Central America, The Far East, and the Middle East, then retired to the Pacific Northwest, USA, where he lives with his wife. He is the author of *In Cellophane of Time, Poems 1973-1987*; *Kottke Ouevre Skookum, 6 and 12-string ears, Vignettes 1970-2019*; and the comic literary novels: *Cutlass Wonders*, *The Ageless of Aquarius*, and *Chronicle of an English Morpheme Addict* published under the series title: *A Measure of Poe & Three Quarters*.

www.ingramcontent.com/pod-product-compliance
Lightning Source LLC
LaVergne TN
LVHW050956080826
845145LV00009B/2323

* 9 7 8 1 7 3 4 5 3 5 6 7 9 *